The Neck

Kezia turned to look at the *Marquis* and the expression in his blue eyes made her feel shy.

"I think we . . . should be . . . going back," she said.

"You cannot always run away," the *Marquis* remarked.

"It is a . . . mistake for us to . . . talk like . . . this," Kezia said.

"What you are really thinking," the *Marquis* replied, "is that you are frightened because we think alike, and it is quite comprehensible to us both."

Because she was suddenly at a loss, and also afraid of her own feelings, Kezia ran away. . . .

A Camfield Novel of Love
by Barbara Cartland

"Barbara Cartland's novels are all distinguished by their intelligence, good sense, and good nature. . . ."
— ROMANTIC TIMES

"Who could give better advice on how to keep your romance going strong than the world's most famous romance novelist, Barbara Cartland?"
— THE STAR

Camfield Place,
Hatfield
Hertfordshire,
England

Dearest Reader,

Camfield Novels of Love mark a very exciting era of my books with Jove. They have already published nearly two hundred of my titles since they became my first publisher in America, and now all my original paperback romances in the future will be published exclusively by them.

As you already know, Camfield Place in Hertfordshire is my home, which originally existed in 1275, but was rebuilt in 1867 by the grandfather of Beatrix Potter.

It was here in this lovely house, with the best view in the country, that she wrote *The Tale of Peter Rabbit*. Mr. McGregor's garden is exactly as she described it. The door in the wall that the fat little rabbit could not squeeze underneath and the goldfish pool where the white cat sat twitching its tail are still there.

I had Camfield Place blessed when I came here in 1950 and was so happy with my husband until he died, and now with my children and grandchildren, that I know the atmosphere is filled with love and we have all been very lucky.

It is easy here to write of love and I know you will enjoy the Camfield Novels of Love. Their plots are definitely exciting and the covers very romantic. They come to you, like all my books, with love:

Bless you,

CAMFIELD NOVELS OF LOVE
by Barbara Cartland

Other Books by Barbara Cartland

A New Camfield Novel of Love by

BARBARA CARTLAND

The Necklace of Love

JOVE BOOKS, NEW YORK

THE NECKLACE OF LOVE

A Jove Book/published by arrangement with
the author

PRINTING HISTORY
Jove edition/May 1990

ISBN: 0-515-10311-X

Jove Books are published by The Berkley Publishing Group,
200 Madison Avenue, New York, New York 10016.
The name "JOVE" and the "J" logo
are trademarks belonging to Jove Publications, Inc.

PRINTED IN THE UNITED STATES OF AMERICA

10 9 8 7 6 5 4 3 2 1

Author's Note

I HAVE seen and touched the necklace I have written about in this novel, which is now in the possession of the Countess of Sutherland. This is the true story of what is wrongly called "The Marie Antoinette Necklace."

The poor unfortunate Queen of France who was to be guillotined never even saw it.

The Comtesse de la Motte, an adventuress descended from a bastard of Henry II, intrigued to procure the necklace pretending it was for Queen Marie Antoinette, but in reality it was for herself.

An enormous and magnificent diamond necklace worth 1,600,000 *livres*, it had twenty-one huge diamonds in a collet round the neck and four long strands, each containing hundreds of diamonds falling from it and ending in enormous tassels of diamonds.

The Comtesse tricked Prince Louis de Rohan, Cardinal and Head Chaplain of France, into believing that the Queen wished to acquire it surreptitiously, and he agreed to help her.

When a servant arrived to collect the necklace with the forged signature of the Queen, Cardinal Rohan was deceived into believing it was genuine, and handed him the diamond necklace.

The jeweller claimed his money for the necklace and Queen Marie Antoinette disclaimed all knowledge of it. Eventually the truth came out.

The Comtesse de la Motte was sentenced to be flogged and branded on each shoulder with a "V" (*Voleuse* — thief).

Taking with her the 21 large diamonds from the collet of the Necklace, the Comtesse escaped to London, where she sold the diamonds. She died in 1791.

Cardinal Rohan was acquitted of the charge of fraud, but was deprived of his offices and banished.

This incident gravely discredited and weakened the French Monarchy and was particularly responsible from the beginning for the violence of the Revolution.

The Necklace of Love

chapter one

1839

KEZIA, looking out of the window, saw a Phaeton coming down the drive and gave a cry of delight.

She ran along the passage and down the beautifully carved oak staircase into the hall.

She flung open the door just as her brother pulled his horses to a standstill.

"Perry!" she exclaimed. "I was not expecting you. How exciting!"

Sir Peregrine Falcon handed his reins to a groom and stepped from the Phaeton.

As he reached the steps his sister ran down them and flung her arms round his neck.

"It is wonderful you are back!" she exclaimed.

"You are ruining my cravat!" her brother protested, but he was smiling.

They walked into the hall together.

"But why have you come home?" she asked. "What

1

has happened? You said you would not be back for weeks.''

"I have some news which I think will please you," Perry replied, "but first I would like something to drink.''

Kezia hesitated.

"I am afraid there is only some claret which I was keeping for your return, or cider.''

"Cider will do," Perry replied, "and we will need the claret.''

She looked at him in surprise but he did not explain, and she ran to the kitchen quarters.

Humber, the old Butler who had served her father for forty years before he died, was sitting in the Pantry.

He was polishing the silver, and his leg, which was stiff with arthritis, was propped up on a stool.

"Sir Peregrine is back!" Kezia said excitedly. "And he wants a glass of cider. Do not move, just tell me where it is.''

"It's just at the top of the cellar, Miss Kezia, where it keeps cool," Humber replied.

He did not attempt to move to fetch it.

If his master was back, it meant he would have to wait at dinner, and he could move only with difficulty.

Kezia ran to the cellar door, opened it, and found, as Humber had told her, that there were several kegs of home-made cider brewed by one of the Farmers on the estate.

She took the nearest and carried it back, knowing that her brother would have gone into the Library, which was the room they used when they were alone.

It had at one time been very impressive, but now the curtains were faded, the chairs needed repairing, and the carpet was threadbare in places.

Because her father had always kept a grog-tray in a corner of the Library with drink on it for anyone who needed it,

Peregrine, when he had come into the Baronetcy, had continued the habit.

Now there were no decanters or bottles, only two or three glasses, so that there was plenty of room for Kezia to put the keg of cider down on the tray.

Her brother pulled out the cork.

"The roads were incredibly dusty today," he said, "but I managed the journey in three hours, which I consider a record!"

"Is that counting your stop for luncheon," Kezia asked, "or are you hungry?"

She looked at him anxiously, thinking there was little in the house. Humber's wife, Betsy, who did the cooking, would be resting.

"No, I had something to eat," Perry replied, "and I deducted that from the time I left London until I reached here. To be truthful, in exactly three hours, sixteen minutes, and a few seconds!"

Kezia laughed.

"No wonder you feel proud!"

"I have something more important to be proud of," Perry said.

Kezia looked at him questioningly, wondering what had happened and feeling a little apprehensive.

Things had been so difficult lately.

They were so hard up that she was always afraid her brother, whom she loved very dearly, would marry for wealth rather than because he was in love.

Although he was an impoverished Baronet, it would not be difficult, considering how handsome he was.

He was very much in demand simply because he was charming, good-mannered, and contributed to the gaiety of every party he attended.

He was also an outstanding rider, so that men liked him, while women became infatuated with him.

Even so, Kezia knew how humiliating it was that his friends were all richer than he was.

While he accepted a great deal of hospitality, it was impossible for him to return it.

In the past, some of his closest friends had come to stay, but he could not provide them with beautiful women to entertain them, nor the horses they rode when their host had large stables.

Kezia was therefore alone week after week, month after month, in the attractive but dilapidated black and white house that had been in the Falcon family for generations.

It had been there since the Falcons had moved from Cornwall, where the family had started, because Surrey was closer to London.

They had found Surrey much more amusing than living, as Kezia's father had once said, "at the very end of the world!"

Nevertheless, Kezia had always felt that, as her name was Cornish, she really belonged there.

As she waited for her brother to explain why he had come, she looked very lovely.

Her gown, which she had made herself, had been washed until it had lost a great deal of its colour, and because she had worn it for several years, it had also become too tight over her curved breasts.

But that did not detract from the gold in her hair with its red tints which caught the sunshine coming through the Library windows.

Her eyes, which were green, seemed also to catch the sunlight as she waited to hear what Perry had to tell her.

He drank half the glass of cider before he said:

"Now, hold your breath! I think I have sold the neck-lace!"

Kezia gave a little gasp, then exclaimed:

"Are you sure? Are you going to get what you were asking for it?"

"I am practically certain that when the *Marquis* sees it, he will not only buy it, but pay exactly the sum I want."

"The *Marquis*?" Kezia questioned.

Perry took another sip of the cider before he said:

"The *Marquis* de Bayeux."

"French!" Kezia murmured.

"Norman!" her brother corrected her.

"But how do you know him, and how did you manage to tell him about the necklace?"

"I first met the *Marquis* a year ago when he was buying horses at Tattersalls," Perry explained. "I have seen him on and off at Race-Meetings, as he often comes to England. Then two days ago, one of my friends, Harry Perceval— you remember Harry?"

"Yes, of course!" Kezia answered.

"Well, Harry brought him to Whites Club, and as he entered I heard somebody behind me say:

" 'I saw Bayeux in Bond Street this afternoon, buying diamonds for a beautiful creature who was already weighted down with them!' "

Perry paused.

"It was then it struck me he might be just the person we were looking for."

Kezia clasped her hands together.

"Oh, Perry, I hope you are right! We need the money so desperately, and as you have said so often, it would be foolish to accept the ridiculously small sum the Jewellers offered us."

"If the *Marquis* comes up to scratch," Perry said, "it will certainly have been worthwhile waiting for the right man to come along, even though it has been extremely uncomfortable at times."

He looked round the room, taking in at a glance how shabby it was. Then he looked at his sister.

"It is you who has suffered worst," he said frankly, "and I swear, Kezia, I will make it up to you. You shall come to London, have pretty gowns, and we will get one of our relations to present you at Buckingham Palace."

"It sounds wonderful!" Kezia said. "At the same time, I think I would rather have a decent horse to ride than a gown in which to dance!"

"You shall have both!" Perry answered. "But now, as the *Marquis* is arriving in two days time, you have to disappear."

Kezia looked at her brother in astonishment.

"What do you mean . . . disappear?"

"What I say," Perry replied.

"But . . . I do not . . . understand."

"Well, *Monsieur le Marquis* is not only a very wealthy man and owns a great deal of property in Normandy—I believe his *Château* is magnificent—but he also has a house in Paris, which is as notorious as he is himself."

"He is notorious for what?" Kezia asked.

Perry hesitated for a moment. Then he said:

"For running after women. He has broken more hearts than Casanova, and is such a '*Don Juan*' that no woman is safe with him!"

"So that is why you will not let me see him!"

"Exactly!" Perry said. "You are too young, too innocent, and much too pretty!"

Kezia laughed.

"How can you be so ridiculous? If the *Marquis* has, as you say, pursued lovely women in France, he is not likely to look at me."

"I see your point," Perry admitted, "at the same time, he is dangerous."

" 'Forewarned is forearmed!' " Kezia quoted.

"It is not only what the *Marquis* will do," Perry said, "but Harry was telling me that he has some strange charisma about him which makes women throw themselves at his feet. According to Harry, he has only to look at them, and they behave like lunatics!"

Kezia laughed again.

"I do not believe a word of it!" she said. "Even if the *Marquis* did look at me, which is very unlikely, he sounds the sort of man who would frighten me! So I would be too busy running away from him to do anything so foolish as to fall in love with him!"

"You cannot be certain of that," Perry said, "so you understand that you must go away for the two days he is here."

"And who is going to look after him?" Kezia asked.

"It is not only him."

"He is bringing somebody else?"

"He is, and I call it impertinent and almost an insult, but I can hardly object."

"What are you saying?" Kezia asked.

"The *Marquis* left a note for me at Whites Club to say he would be coming here on Thursday, bringing with him a *Madame* de Salres."

"Who is she?"

"She is his current . . ."

Here Perry stopped, realising that what he had been about to say would have been indiscreet.

7

After a pause he went on:

"I understand she is a—very close friend."

"What you are saying is that she is in love with him!" Kezia said. "Well, that makes it quite clear that he will not notice me, and I am sure if the *Marquis* is interested enough to bring a Lady-friend with him, he is definitely enamoured of her."

"That is very likely true," Perry agreed reluctantly. "At the same time, he has no right to bring her into the house when you are present."

"But, you have said, I will not be here," Kezia remarked logically. "You obviously did not tell him I would be acting as hostess."

Perry put down his empty glass.

"There is no use in arguing about it," he said firmly. "You must stay away. Perhaps you could stay with some friends, or with the Vicar in the village."

"Surely the Vicar would think it very strange if I ask him if I can stay with him because you are entertaining a man of whom you do not approve?" Kezia said. "And you know we cannot say that we are selling the necklace, or it might get into the newspapers."

Perry frowned.

"Oh, stop making difficulties," he said, "there must be somewhere you can go!"

"And what do you think will happen if I do?" Kezia asked. "You know who we have in the house—Old Humber, whose rheumatics are so bad he can only just shuffle into the Dining-Room."

She paused, then went on:

"While Betsy is a good cook, she cannot manage anything complicated, and certainly not a dish that would be palatable to a Frenchman!"

Perry was listening with a frown between his eyes, but he did not interrupt as Kezia went on:

"You know Mrs. Jones comes in from the village for two hours every day, but she could not manage the beds without me, and she forgets what she is supposed to do unless I remind her."

Kezia paused, and Perry said irritably:

"Well, try to find somebody else."

"And train them in two days? You know that is impossible!"

"Nothing is impossible," Perry said crossly, "and if we lose the *Marquis*, we may never find another buyer for the necklace."

"Why can he not see it in London?" Kezia asked.

"Because when I told him it had been in our possession ever since the 1789 Revolution, I happened to mention that my grandfather had bought it for my grandmother to wear when she was painted by Reynolds.

" 'That is something I must see!' the *Marquis* exclaimed. 'I have several Reynolds in my Collection, and consider him one of the best English artists there has ever been, especially when it came to painting women.'

" 'I agree with you,' I said, and it was then he asked himself to stay."

"I see you could hardly take the picture to London when it is so large!" Kezia agreed.

"What was I to do," Perry asked, "except agree that he come here, but I had no idea he was going to bring some fastidious Frenchwoman with him!"

Kezia gave a little cry.

"If she is fastidious, and therefore uncomfortable, she may persuade him to leave earlier than he intends, and not buy the necklace."

9

Perry saw the point of what his sister was saying and walked across the room to the window.

He looked out at the garden, which had grown very wild with no-one to tend it.

"I have been planning all the way down here," he said, as if he spoke to himself, "the improvements we can make to the house. To start with, we have to mend the roof and put new panes of glass in the windows."

"We need a new stove in the kitchen," Kezia said. "It is a miracle the old one has lasted as long as it has, and if you do not do something about the pump, we shall have no water unless we fetch it from the lake."

"I know, I know!" Perry groaned. "That is why we have to make sure that the *Marquis* is satisfied not only with the necklace, but also with the house and the food he eats."

"Therefore," Kezia said positively, "you cannot do without me!"

Perry put his hand up to his forehead.

"I am trying to look after you," he said. "I am trying to make sure that you do not make a fool of yourself over a man who will go back to France and forget you even exist!"

Kezia threw up her hands.

"What can I say to convince you that I will not fall in love with him? All I will do is to make him so comfortable and feed him so well that he will be in a good humour and pay up!"

Perry walked back to stand in front of the fireplace.

He was looking at his sister as if he had never seen her before, and he said:

"You know, if you were decently dressed and your hair were done in a fashionable manner, you would be a sensation in London!"

"Thank you, Dearest!" Kezia said. "It is very nice of you to talk like that, but you know as well as I do that unless we sell the necklace, I will never go to London, and the only people who are likely to think me a sensation here are Humber, Betsy, the rooks, and the rabbits!"

Perry laughed.

"That is true enough, anyway! But I have the uncomfortable feeling that if I let you stay, however reasonable it sounds, it is something I shall bitterly regret!"

Because he sounded so anxious, Kezia rose from the sofa on which she had been sitting and went to his side.

She kissed his cheek before she said:

"You are a wonderful brother, and you have always been very kind to me, but now you have to trust me."

"I trust you," Perry said. "It is that damned Frenchman I do not trust any further than I can see him!"

There was silence, and he realised his sister was looking shocked because he had sworn.

"I am sorry," he said. "I only wish to God Mama were here. She would know how to cope with him."

"Of course she would," Kezia said softly.

Then she gave a sudden cry.

"I have an idea!"

Perry walked again to the window, then turned his head back to ask:

"What is it?"

"It is what you said just now about Mama being here. If Mama and Papa were entertaining the *Marquis* and the fastidious Frenchwoman he is bringing with him, there would be no difficulty."

"Of course not," Perry agreed, "except that I think Mama would have been rather shocked that they were travelling together without a chaperon."

He thought to himself, although he did not say it out loud, that it was damned insulting of the Frenchman to bring his mistress into a respectable household.

But it was something he could not say to Kezia.

"My idea," Kezia was saying slowly, "is that I should be your wife!"

There was silence while her brother stared at her.

"What are you saying?"

"You think that the *Marquis* will make advances to me because I am an unattached woman, but he would not dare approach me if I were his hostess and your wife!"

It shot through Perry's mind that the fact that Kezia was married would not inhibit the *Marquis* as she thought it would.

Madame de Salres doubtless had a husband who had been left behind in Paris.

At the same time, he saw it would certainly make things better if Kezia were a "married woman," provided that they had not been married for long.

Kezia was waiting, and Perry thought over very carefully what she had said before he replied cautiously:

"It is a possibility!"

"It is a sensible solution!" Kezia corrected him. "I can stay here and look after him. I can make sure what servants we do have will carry out their duties, and I assure you I shall be too busy doing all that besides coping with most of the cooking to philander with the *Marquis*, however attractive he may be!"

"I shall certainly be a very jealous husband!" Perry remarked.

Kezia clapped her hands together.

"Of course you will, and he could hardly be so thick-skinned as to flirt with me in front of you!"

Perry did not reply, and she went on:

"Besides, if he is busy with *Madame* de Salres, why should he take any notice of me?"

Perry wondered why he had not thought of that himself.

At the same time, he was suddenly aware that his sister seemed even more beautiful than she had when he had last been home.

The Falcon women were famous for their beauty all down the centuries, and there was plenty of evidence of it in the portraits of them which hung on the walls.

As he remembered that, he gave an exclamation and said:

"The idea is hopeless!"

"Why?" Kezia asked.

"Because you are very like the portrait of Mama which hangs in the Drawing-Room, and Papa always said you resemble the wife of the fourth Baronet, who was acclaimed as a great beauty by all the officers who fought with Marlborough!"

Kezia thought for a moment, then she said:

"Then I am a cousin, and I was also a Falcon, and we fell in love because we have known each other since we were children."

"I suppose that might be the explanation," Perry said doubtfully.

"It is a sensible one if you think about it," Kezia said, "and if the *Marquis* is interested in the house, I should have to know all about the Falcons."

She paused to smile at him before continuing:

"It is reasonable, therefore, to explain that as a Falcon myself I was brought up on the history of the family, their ghosts, and, of course, the 'Bad Baronet,' who is responsible for our present predicament!"

Perry did not speak, and after a moment Kezia went on:

"As I have told you before, I shall be delighted if we can sell the necklace. I have always believed it was unlucky."

"It is going to be lucky for us if the *Marquis* pays the money I am asking for it."

Kezia was not listening.

She was thinking of how the diamond necklace which her grandfather had bought for his wife, had caused the greatest scandal of the eighteenth century.

It was in 1785 that the *Comtesse* de la Motte, an Adventuress, had seen the most expensive and fantastic necklace that had ever been made in Paris.

She had persuaded the Cardinal de Rohan to help her convince the Jeweller that the necklace was to be given to Queen Marie-Antoinette.

Instead, the *Comtesse* had stolen it, and her subsequent trial had electrified the whole of France.

The *Comtesse* was arrested, but she escaped from prison and fled to London. She took with her twenty-one diamonds she had removed from the necklace.

They were only a small part of what had been the most enormous and magnificent piece of jewellery, besides being the most expensive, of the era.

The diamonds were arranged in a new setting and were very beautiful when they were presented to Lady Falcon, the grandmother of Perry and Kezia.

Because they had caused such a commotion and also so much suffering, many historians averred that the scandal had been directly responsible for the outbreak of the French Revolution.

Kezia, therefore, had always considered them to be unlucky.

They were locked away in a safe place which would have

been difficult for a burglar to locate, and Kezia never put them round her neck.

She did not like to remember that her mother had worn them at a Hunt Ball three months before she died.

It was because the necklace was so valuable that it had been difficult to sell.

Perry had been determined after it had been valued that he would get the right price for it or it would remain where it was.

"It is the one saleable thing we possess," he had said to his sister, "and the only hope we ever have of putting this house back in shape and being able to enjoy ourselves as we should."

Kezia agreed with him, but was aware at the same time that she longed to be able to employ younger and more active servants.

It broke her heart to see the house growing more and more dilapidated month after month.

She loved her home and she loved, too, the old people in the village who were really their responsibility, but for whom they could do so little.

Now, she thought, although there was little time, she must make the *Marquis* and the Frenchwoman with him happy and comfortable.

Otherwise she was quite certain they would leave as quickly as possible without taking the necklace with them.

She felt as if her head were whirling with the thought of all she had to do, but aloud she said:

"Stop wasting time in arguing, Perry! I will be 'Lady Falcon' for the two days the *Marquis* is staying here and I promise you I will be so enraptured with my 'handsome husband,' I will not have time even to look at Satan if he were tempting me with an apple!"

15

"That is exactly what he may be doing!" Perry replied. "And you can understand, however tempting the apple may be, you are to refuse to accept it!"

"I will do exactly as you tell me," Kezia said, "and now we have to get busy."

Perry looked at her questioningly, and she said:

"We need champagne, young lamb from the Farmer, chickens, ducks, and fish."

She smiled before she added:

"There are plenty of trout in the stream, if you can catch them!"

"The only thing I thought of was the champagne!" Perry said. "And that is why I left the Phaeton outside so that I could drive into Guildford at once."

"There are dozens of things I want too," Kezia said, "but your horses will be tired, so I will make a list of them for tomorrow."

Perry walked towards the door.

"I can only hope," he said, "that this deal comes off, otherwise I shall not be able to pay for the champagne or anything else I buy!"

Kezia gave an exclamation of horror.

"Do you mean you are 'below hatches'? Oh, Perry, you have not been gambling again?"

"I was told it was a certainty!" he said bitterly, going from the Library and slamming the door behind him.

Kezia put her hand up to her head.

She knew what lay in front of her was going to be a gigantic task.

It meant that besides getting the house ready, she would have to cook a large number of the more important dishes that Betsy would be incapable of managing.

It was a blessing that it was early Summer, and therefore not every course would have to be hot.

But if Betsy grew very tired, there would be too many things to be done at the same time.

She also had to impress upon Betsy and Humber that they were not to address her as "Miss Kezia" as was usual, but as "M'Lady."

"And all this," she said beneath her breath, "for a Frenchman who will not appreciate any of it, but take it as a matter of course!"

Also he and his fastidious friend would doubtless disparage the way she looked and look down on the house.

For a moment she felt humiliated, then she put up her chin defiantly.

She was a Falcon, and however rich the *Marquis* might be, her blood was as good, if not better, than his.

He might be, for all she knew, a descendant of William the Conqueror, but the Falcons were living in Cornwall before he invaded England.

The History-Books said there were Falcons who fought with King Harold at the Battle of Hastings.

"If the *Marquis* thinks he can trample on Perry and me, he is going to be mistaken!" she told herself. "And I will make it quite clear when he arrives that we speak to him as equals."

Then, as she walked towards the door, she saw a reflection of herself in the one gilt mirror hanging on the wall.

It showed her quite clearly how unfashionable and worn her gown was.

She knew very clearly how, if the *Marquis* did not disparage her appearance, any woman, and especially a French one, would be contemptuous, to say the least of it.

"I have to find something decent to wear," Kezia told herself.

She knew she should be going into the kitchen to prepare Betsy for what lay ahead.

Instead, she ran up the stairs and into the room which led off the main bedroom in which her mother had always slept.

It had originally been a Powder-Room, but quite a large one.

Lady Falcon had, however, converted it into a room where she kept all her clothes.

"I have always thought it unnecessary and very unromantic," she had said, "to keep one's clothes in a bedroom, unless it is absolutely necessary."

She had, therefore, made it so beautiful that it was more like a Sitting-Room.

"Wardrobes are ugly pieces of furniture!" she had said.

They were, therefore, banished to the Powder-Room, which had not been used since the end of the previous century.

Because, after her mother had died, Kezia had kept her room almost sacred, nobody had stayed in it and she seldom bothered to enter the Powder-Room, where her mother's clothes still remained.

Once or twice when she had either grown out of her own clothes or they had fallen to bits, she had thought she would find something that had belonged to her.

For the last two years, however, there had been no necessity for her to look anything but what she called a "Beggar-maid" in her own garments.

When Perry came home he came alone, and after the period of mourning was over the neighbours seemed to have forgotten that she was there and seldom sent her invitations.

There was no money for horses, so she could not hunt in the Winter.

The old horses who carried her to the farms when she called on their tenants or went down to the village were reliable.

They were so slow, however, that she usually preferred to walk rather than ride.

Now, as she entered her mother's Wardrobe-Room, there was the fragrance of the white violet perfume which Lady Falcon had distilled every Spring.

There was also the scent of lavender in the little muslin bags she had made and put in the linen cupboard, and amongst her under-garments.

For a moment the perfume brought back her mother so vividly that Kezia felt the tears come into her eyes.

Then she told herself severely that there was no time for sentimentality.

She just had to look to see if there was anything she could wear in which to entertain the *Marquis*.

If, as she suspected, her mother's gowns would make her look older, and were not appropriate for a very young girl, that was exactly what she wanted.

She opened the doors of the wardrobe and for a moment the kaleidoscope of soft colours seemed to blind her eyes.

Then, as impatiently she brushed away the tears, she saw there were several gowns in which she could play the part of Perry's wife.

Her mother's dressing-table stood beside the window, and she sat down for a moment on the stool to look at herself in the mirror.

Then she did not see her own face, but her mother's, and she said in her heart:

"Help me, Mama . . . and help us to sell the necklace

which will give Perry so many things he wants and restore the house to the way it ought to look, instead of the state it is in now."

Kezia had the strange feeling that it was her mother who smiled back at her rather than her own reflection.

Then she jumped to her feet, shut the doors of the wardrobe, and, opening the door, ran as quickly as she could along the passage and down the stairs.

There was so much to do, and she must not waste a moment.

She knew it was only by a superhuman effort that she would be ready for the notorious *Marquis* when he arrived.

"And when he does," Kezia told herself, "I shall be so exhausted by everything that has to be done that if he is, as Perry says, a modern Casanova, there will be nothing he can do or say that will get the slightest response from me!"

She was laughing at her own joke as she pushed open the baize door which needed recovering and which led into the kitchen quarters.

Old Humber was in the Pantry cleaning the few silver dishes which she and Perry used when they were alone.

Kezia wondered frantically if he would ever have time to clean the candelabra that were to be put on the table at dinner.

There were also *entrée* dishes, the coffee-pot, sugar bowl and cream jug, besides the salvers which were used whenever they had guests staying in the house.

"The whole thing is impossible!" she told herself despondently.

Then once again her pride told her that there was no such word and what had to be done must be done and the sooner the better.

Old Humber, still with his leg on a stool, looked up and waited for her to speak.

The sunshine coming through the window showed up what was left of his white hair and the lines on his face.

The gnarled fingers of his hand which held the tea-pot were swollen with rheumatism.

In a voice that sounded even to herself weak and inaudible, Kezia said:

"I . . . I have something to . . . tell you, Humber . . . and it is very important!"

chapter two

KEZIA hurried into the Breakfast-Room to find Perry eating his breakfast.

"I am sorry to be late," she said breathlessly, "but there has been such a lot to do."

She had been up since six o'clock tidying the Drawing-Room.

She had also put finishing touches to the bedrooms which would be occupied by the *Marquis* de Bayeux and *Madame* de Salres.

She had been rather surprised when Perry had said to her:

"Put our guests next door to each other."

Kezia had raised her eyes.

"Next door?" she asked. "I thought *Madame* de Salres would appreciate the Rose Room, which, after Mama's, is, I always think, the most beautiful room in the house."

It was her mother who had christened the rooms with the names of flowers.

She had tried where possible to have the colours of them in the curtains, the cushions and, because they had a large collection, the pictures.

"That is a mistake," Perry said. "If you put the *Marquis* in the Water-Lily Room which overlooks the garden, then *Madame* de Salres must be next door."

"I cannot imagine why!" Kezia said.

Perry thought how he could offer her an explanation. Then he said:

"She might feel lonely or afraid in a strange house where there are few people."

"Oh, of course!" Kezia agreed. "I never thought of that! Then she will have to go into the Lilac Room, which is very pretty."

"I am sure that would suit her," Perry said with relief.

The room, however, had not been used for some time.

Although Mrs. Jones had cleaned it perfunctorily, Kezia found there was a great deal for her to do to make it as comfortable as she was sure the Frenchwoman would expect.

Now, as she sat down at the table, Perry took up a letter which was lying by his place and looked at it, frowning.

"What is . . . it?" Kezia asked anxiously.

She had a sudden fear that after all their optimism the *Marquis* had changed his mind and was not coming to stay.

There was a pause before Perry said:

"This is a letter from the *Marquis*' Secretary, who informs me that he will be arriving at about five o'clock."

"That is a sensible hour!" Kezia said with relief. "As he is French, he will not expect tea, and after you have given them something to drink, *Madame*, at any rate, can rest before dinner.''

''I thought that was what you would think,'' her brother replied, ''but the Secretary also says that the *Marquis* will be arriving with a groom, and another carriage will bring down the luggage with his valet and *Madame*'s lady's-maid!''

Kezia gave a little gasp as her brother went on:

''There will also be two outriders!''

''I do not believe it!'' Kezia cried. ''How can two people require five servants with them?''

''I warned you that the *Marquis* considers himself of great importance, and he is rich enough to afford five-hundred attendants if he needs them!''

''But . . . how can we possibly . . . accommodate all those people?'' Kezia asked helplessly.

''We cannot!'' Perry said firmly. ''The outriders and the groom must stay at The Fox and Hounds.''

''They will be very uncomfortable there,'' Kezia murmured.

''We shall have to accommodate the lady's-maid and the valet,'' Perry went on as if she had not spoken, ''and I should have thought of that before!''

''I suppose I should have too,'' Kezia said, ''but it is so long since Mama could afford a lady's maid, and you have never had a valet, so I forgot.''

''So did I, to be honest,'' Perry said, ''but they will have to be in the house.''

''There are plenty of bedrooms, as you know,'' Kezia said, ''but it means cleaning them all out and making the beds, and I have so many other things to do.''

''Surely Betsy can help you?'' Perry suggested.

''Betsy is already collapsing,'' Kezia answered, ''and

although Jenny, the girl I have got from the village, is doing her best, she had not the slightest idea of what she is expected to do and is often more trouble than she is worth!''

Perry looked at the letter again, then slipped it into the pocket of his coat.

''Why was I such a fool as to let the *Marquis* persuade me to invite him here?'' he enquired.

''You must not blame yourself,'' Kezia said quickly. ''We will manage somehow. But if servants are uncomfortable they always grumble, and that may upset the *Marquis*.''

Perry did not answer, he only rose from his chair and said:

''I am now going to inspect the stables to see if they are decent enough for his horses. I expected two, and now he is bringing four!''

''Perhaps you will have the chance of riding one of them,'' Kezia said.

But she did not think her brother heard her, for he had already left the Breakfast-Room.

She rose from the table and, picking up the plates and cups, stacked them onto a tray and carried them into the kitchen.

She told Jenny to wash them up and be very, very careful not to break anything.

''Oi be doin' me best, Miss Kezia!'' she said.

There was a little pile of broken crockery already on the dresser, and Kezia thought with a sigh that unless the *Marquis* bought the necklace, they would never be replaced.

She went upstairs to find Mrs. Jones and asked her to clean out the two rooms in which the lady's-maid and the valet would sleep.

She had intended to put them in the Servants' Quarters

on the second floor which had always been used in the past, but then she had an idea.

There were two Bachelor Rooms which were not as impressive or as elaborate as the State-Rooms.

They had been used before her father died when he had friends who came only for one night, usually to hunt the next day.

"I will put the servants in those," she decided, "and at least the beds are comfortable and the rooms in fairly good repair."

When she and Mrs. Jones looked at them, she found, however, that soot had fallen down one chimney, making a mess on the hearth-rug.

Owing to a crack in one of the window panes, starlings had nested in the other.

By the time all this had been cleaned up it was time for luncheon, and Perry was shouting for her up the stairs.

It was a rather sparse meal, but she thought it was a mistake to ask Betsy to cook anything before dinner tonight.

Everything that was cold she had already cooked herself and arranged the dishes carefully so that all Old Humber had to do was to bring them into the Dining-Room.

She knew she could trust Betsy with the leg of lamb. She herself had picked the new peas from the garden and the smallest of the new potatoes which, with plenty of butter, would be very palatable.

There was also asparagus rather thin and wild, which would be served with the main course.

By four o'clock Kezia was feeling as if her legs would no longer carry her, and what she wanted to do more than anything else was to lie down.

She had arranged most of the flowers the day before,

and they made all the difference to the Drawing-Room, which had not been opened for so long.

She had also put a large bowl in the hall, and it made a vivid touch of colour against the darkness of the walls and the carved oak staircase.

Because it was what her mother would have done, she had put waters-lilies that were just coming into flower in the *Marquis*' bedroom.

Next, because the white lilac was over, she put a vase of lilies in *Madame* de Salres' bedroom.

She had also added a bowl of white roses and thought that, against the mauve curtains, they made the room look lovely.

"I only hope she is grateful for all the trouble we have taken!" Kezia said to herself, then laughed.

She was quite certain, coming from Paris—or was it the *Marquis*' *Château* in Normandy—that *Madame* de Salres would undoubtedly disparage anything so simple as an English country home.

Especially, she thought, one which needed an enormous amount of money spent on it to make it look as it was in the old days.

When she reached her bedroom she remembered because there had been so much to do that she had not decided in which of her mother's gowns she would receive the *Marquis*.

She had already chosen the one she would wear in the evening, which was of emerald green gauze so that it did not need pressing.

Kezia knew that if she had to keep the irons on the kitchen stove it would interfere with the cooking.

Besides, Betsy grew agitated if there were too many people around her.

Now Kezia opened the wardrobe.

Because the gowns reminded her how much she missed her mother, for a moment she had an impulse not to wear them.

She could meet the *Marquis* in one of her own out-grown, over-washed gowns.

Then she knew she would be letting Perry down.

If the *Marquis* was as formidable as he feared, she should try to charm him into a good temper, otherwise the whole visit would be a disaster.

She therefore took from its hanger a gown she had always loved to see her mother in because it was the blue of forget-me-nots, and also the colour of her mother's eyes.

Kezia was undoubtedly like Lady Falcon. But her eyes were a different hue, and her hair was a little more red.

Lady Falcon had actually had the colouring that foreigners often described as a "Perfect English Rose," and Kezia thought it was a pity that she was different.

Perhaps, she thought, if the *Marquis* noticed her at all, he would not admire her.

There was, however, no time to worry, and she hurried to her bedroom and put on the gown, which was slightly out-of-date.

Skirts had grown much larger in the last two years.

The young Queen had set the fashion for evening-gowns which were off the shoulders, waists which were tiny, and skirts that flared out over what appeared to be a multitude of petticoats.

Lady Falcon's gown was far more restrained, after the fashion set by Queen Adelaide, who had always been extremely prim and proper.

Yet because Kezia was so thin, her waist was tiny, and

although the skirts should have been larger, the whole gown revealed the grace of her figure.

Also, although she did not realise it, it made her look very young.

She had no time to arrange her hair in a fashionable manner, but just parted it in the centre and secured it at the back of her head.

Then when she was about to examine her reflection in the mirror to see if there was any way by which she could improve her appearance, she heard Perry call her from downstairs:

"Kezia! Where are you? They are turning to the drive!"

Running as quickly as she could along the passage, Kezia reached the top of the stairs.

Now she could see through one of the windows in the hall that there were horses crossing the bridge over the lake.

Even at that distance she realised they were a magnificent team, perfectly matched and jet-black.

The man driving them had a top-hat on the side of his head.

When they drew nearer she could see there was a Lady beside him wearing a bonnet on which fluttered a number of feathers.

Then, as she stood there staring, Perry said:

"Hurry up, you should be in the Drawing-Room! I will wait in the hall."

As he spoke, Humber, in his long-tailed coat, came shuffling from under the stairs towards the front door.

Kezia had a quick glimpse of two outriders just behind the Phaeton and thought their horses looked unusually fine.

She reached the hall and, running past Perry, hurried into the Drawing-Room.

Her heart was beating and she felt breathless.

It was only because of the speed at which she had hurried down the stairs, and because now that the *Marquis* was actually arriving, she felt frightened.

So much depended on his visit.

If anything went wrong, she was aware that there would be more bills to meet than there had been a week ago, and she had no idea how they could pay them.

She had found a man in the village who had come up to help Humber and who would carry the luggage upstairs.

He had been in service when he was young, but he had now gone into partnership with the Blacksmith.

He did not wish to go back to the days when he was, as he said, a slave taking orders from anyone who wished to give them.

It was only because Kezia's father had always been kind to him when he gave a hand during the Hunting Season that he now condescended to come to the house for the two nights the *Marquis* was staying with them.

"Oi b'ain't wearin' no livery, Miss!" he said firmly.

"No, of course not!" Kezia said quickly, although she hoped that was what he would do. "If you will just carry the dishes to the Dining-Room door so that Humber can take them in, and look after our guest's valet, I would be very, very grateful."

She pleaded with him so prettily that it would have taken a heart of stone to refuse her.

Douglas, somewhat reluctantly, had agreed to help.

Of course she promised to pay him more than she would have paid somebody completely untrained.

It would be worth it if the "end justified the means."

'If the *Marquis* does not buy the necklace,' Kezia thought in a panic, 'then we shall have to find something else to sell.'

The pictures as well as the furniture would all be entailed onto the son which Perry had said he would never be able to afford.

Now, waiting for the *Marquis* to arrive, Kezia found herself praying that he would buy the necklace and, having made up his mind to do so, would leave as soon as possible.

Then, as she heard voices in the hall, she moved a little nearer to the fireplace, thinking it would look less contrived than if she stood near the door.

She could hear Perry talking, and now, although he sounded at his ease, underneath she knew he was tense and anxious.

Then there was a deep voice answering him, and a moment later the door opened.

It was *Madame* de Salres who came in first, and the moment Kezia saw her she felt her heart sink.

Never had she imagined any woman could look so smart, although she was aware that "*chic*" was the right word.

She wore also fantastic jewellery in a manner that did not make it look vulgar or over-powering.

For a moment Kezia had no eyes for the man who walked behind her.

As *Madame* de Salres moved almost like a ship in full sail down the Drawing-Room, she advanced a little way to meet her.

"May I present my wife," she heard Perry say.

As she curtsied, *Madame* de Salres held out an exquisitely gloved hand.

"I do hope you have had a good journey," Kezia said in her soft voice.

"*Non*, eet was *abominable*," *Madame* replied. "The dust in your country eez—'ow do you say?—a cloud of darkness, and I am enveloped in eet!"

She spoke as though it were Kezia's fault.

Then a voice from behind her said in perfect English, except for a slight accent:

"As usual, Yvonne, you exaggerate your suffering, although I, too, am delighted to arrive at my destination!"

For a moment Kezia could not look at the *Marquis* even though she thought his voice was attractive.

Then, as she curtsied, he raised her hand perfunctorily to his lips, and as she lifted her eyes she found he was not in the least what she had expected.

She had somehow had a picture in her mind that being French he would be dark, small, and perhaps because of what Perry had said about him, somehow like the Devil in the Picture-Books.

Instead, he was taller than Perry, with broad shoulders and the narrow hips of an athlete.

His hair was certainly dark, but astonishingly, until she remembered he came from Normandy, his eyes were blue.

They were not the blue of her mother's, which had been like the blue of a Summer sky, but the dark blue of the sea.

For a moment she was so surprised that she could not speak.

Then, as she looked at him, she realised there was a slightly mocking smile on his lips.

It gave him an unexpectedly cynical expression which was out of keeping with the rest of his face.

"It is very kind of you to have us to stay," the *Marquis* said. "As I expect your husband has told you, I am very eager to see the necklace, and also your pictures."

"I hope you will not be disappointed," Perry said before Kezia could speak. "I hear your own Collection is magnificent."

"I like to think so," the *Marquis* said, "but there is

always room for improvement, as I am sure you yourself find.''

: "Yes, of course,'' Perry said hastily. "And now, let me give you some refreshment, and I am sure nothing would be more suitable than the wine of your own country.''

He turned to the side table, where Kezia had put the wine-cooler that Humber had sat up half the night polishing.

In it was a bottle of champagne which Perry had bought yesterday.

Perry poured out two glasses and carried one to *Madame* de Salres, who had seated herself rather disdainfully, Kezia thought, on the sofa.

She was spreading out her skirt to accentuate the fullness of it.

"A glass of champagne eez something I certainly need!'' she said. "My throat eez so dry I can 'ardly croak!''

"Then drink quickly,'' the *Marquis* said, "so that your dulcet tones which you have often told me resemble that of a nightingale can be heard in this attractive house which I am sure has a dozen nightingales in the garden.''

Kezia laughed.

"We have a few,'' she admitted, "but many more rooks and crows, as is usual in England.''

The *Marquis* took a sip from his glass. Then he said:

"Tell me about your home, *Madame* Falcon. From what I have seen of it already, I find it charming! I imagine it was built in the reign of Charles II.''

"That is clever of you,'' Kezia exclaimed. "It was built after the Restoration, when the Falcon of the day was spared being executed in the Tower by a few hours!''

"You must tell me the whole story,'' the *Marquis* said, "and I know I shall find it fascinating.''

There was something in the way he spoke which made

Kezia realise that in an obscure manner he was paying her a compliment.

She blushed, then, turning to Perry, said:

"Have you explained, Dearest, that the coachman and the outriders have to go to The Fox and Hounds."

She saw as she spoke that Perry had forgotten, and he said quickly:

"No, but I will go and do so at once while you explain to the *Marquis* how sorry we arc that we cannot accommodate them."

Kezia drew in her breath.

"I hope . . . you will . . . not mind," she said apologetically, "but as we are very short-staffed and as our servants are old, we could not at such short notice have so . . . many people here . . . in the house."

"I quite understand," the *Marquis* said, "and it is something I should have thought of myself."

"No . . . no . . . of course not! Why should you?" Kezia said. "And I am sure the Landlord of the Inn will make them comfortable."

She had, in fact, called on Mr. Geary, the Landlord of The Fox and Hounds, when she had gone into the village for provisions.

She had begged him to do what he could for the *Marquis'* servants.

"Ye knows we bain't be used t'visitors, Miss," the old man had replied, "an' the Missus don't 'ave much toim t'keep the rooms as they should be."

"I know it is late to ask you," Kezia said quickly.

"Well, Oi'll do me best. Oi'll gi' 'em a bed, but wot do they plan t'eat?" Mr. Geary said. "Ye knows well as Oi do they'd be more comfort'ble up at t'house."

"We just cannot manage to look after any more people,"

Kezia said, "so please, Mr. Geary, help us. It is very, very important that they should not be uncomfortable and in consequence disagreeable."

Mr. Geary laughed.

"Oi can't say 'no' to ye, Miss, 'avin' known ye since ye were a little 'un, but Oi can't do more'n me best, an' that's all Oi can say."

Kezia thought it was what she might say too.

Now she was afraid that if the *Marquis* was annoyed, everything might go wrong.

Hastily, to make everything better she said:

"I promise that your horses will be comfortable."

There was a twist to the *Marquis*' lips as he said:

"I think, Lady Falcon, you are offering me a chocolate to take away the taste of the medicine."

Kezia laughed.

"That is what I always had as a child."

"I did too," the *Marquis* said, "but do not worry, I am sure my staff will be comfortable and, if they are not, they will just have to manage."

As if she thought she was being neglected, *Madame* Salres said:

"I shall be uncomfortable until I 'ave washed ze dust out of my 'air. Will you show me my room? I would like to rest before dinner."

"Yes, of course," Kezia replied, "and as we are in the country, we thought you would not mind if we have dinner at seven-thirty."

Madame de Salres held up her hands in horror.

"Seven-thirty!" she exclaimed. "In Paris I nevair dine before nine o'clock."

"You are not in Paris now!" the *Marquis* retorted. "And as I will be hungry, I shall welcome dinner at seven-thirty."

Kezia looked at him gratefully, while *Madame* de Salres with a shrug of her shoulders walked towards the door.

Kezia hurried to follow her, but before she did so she said very quietly to the *Marquis* so that only he could hear:

"Thank . . . you!"

She spoke quite naturally, the way she would have spoken to anybody who had eased the cares of the household.

She did not see the surprise in his blue eyes.

As Kezia took *Madame* de Salres into the Lilac Room, she thought it would be difficult, fastidious though she might be, for her to find fault.

The fragrance of lilies and roses scented the room, and the evening sunshine created a golden glow which looked very attractive.

The luggage had been brought upstairs, and the French lady's-maid had already opened a trunk.

Kezia could see at a glance it was filled with extremely expensive clothes.

"I hope you will find everything you want," she said to *Madame* de Salres.

She was walking around the room as if looking for something with which she could find fault.

As *Madame* did not reply, Kezia said to the lady's-maid in French:

"If there is anything *Madame* requires, please tell me. We will certainly do our best to provide it."

"*Merci*, *Madame*, you are very kind," the lady's-maid replied.

She was a middle-aged woman. Kezia thought she seemed good tempered and hoped she would get on well with Humber and Betsy.

Having no wish to say any more, she went from the room, shutting the door behind her.

Outside, she realised that the door of the Water-Lily Room was open and that the *Marquis'* valet, who looked exactly as she thought a Frenchman should, was unpacking his master's trunk.

She went into the room and said what she had said to the lady's-maid, in French:

"Good afternoon! I hope you will find everything your Master needs, but if not, please tell me."

The Frenchman rose to his feet and bowed.

"*Merci, Madame*," he said, "I am used to accommodating *Monsieur* wherever we find ourselves."

Because he sounded so friendly, Kezia smiled at him as she said: .

"You will understand we live very quietly here and the servants are old, so as I have already said, please come to me if there is anything you want, and I will do my best to provide it."

The Frenchman thanked her again, and because he sounded so sincere and so sensible, she felt less anxious.

But still wondering if Perry required anything, she went downstairs again.

To her surprise, he was not in the Drawing-Room.

The *Marquis* was there alone, standing at the diamond-paned window, looking out onto the garden.

"I thought Perry would be back!" Kezia exclaimed.

"I hope he is admiring my horses," the *Marquis* replied. "I bought them only two days ago, from an old friend, the Duke of Alderstone."

Kezia exclaimed without thinking:

"I know the Duke has some very fine racehorses, but I am surprised he sold you the fine team with which you arrived. I would have expected him to want them for himself."

The *Marquis* smiled.

"Shall I say I made the offer so attractive that he found it impossible to refuse me!"

"Is that what you often do?" Kezia asked curiously.

"When I want something, the price I pay for it is immaterial," the *Marquis* replied. "I am a Norman and I always get what I want."

Kezia sighed.

"It must be marvellous to be as rich as that. At the same time . . . too easy."

"What do you mean—too easy?" the *Marquis* enquired.

Kezia walked to the window.

She was looking out at the garden which, while bright with colour, looked very wild.

"I spoke without thinking," she said after a moment's pause, "but I have learnt how hard it is to be without what one needs and loves, but it is also overwhelmingly exciting if one can achieve what one desires."

"I understand exactly what you are saying," the *Marquis* remarked, "but what do you desire?"

Kezia nearly told him the truth, and wanted to say:

"For you to buy the diamond necklace!"

Then she thought that would be too revealing.

She tried to think of something that would not depend on the money he would give them for it.

To her surprise he read her thoughts.

"Apart from the obvious answer that you are thinking about," he said, "what else?"

She blushed because he was so perceptive, then he said with a cynical note in his voice:

"Surely, unlike most women you cannot say you have everything? Or is it true in your case that true love is enough?"

For a moment Kezia did not understand what he meant.

Then she remembered that she was supposed to be Perry's wife and said quickly:

"You are right . . . of course you are right! If one has love . . . nothing else matters."

As she spoke she looked at the *Marquis* and saw an expression in his eyes.

She had a feeling that this was just the sort of conversation which Perry had warned her about.

Hastily, because she was embarrassed, she said:

"I must go to get ready for dinner, and please, although I am sure it is an incorrect thing to say . . . do not be . . . late."

She thought he looked surprised and added:

"I have taken so much trouble over the menu, and if the dishes are spoilt, it will be a disaster!"

The *Marquis* laughed, and it was a spontaneous sound.

"I will not be late," he promised.

Because she felt she was saying all the wrong things, she ran from the room, shutting the door behind her.

Then, to her relief, she saw that Perry was coming in through the open front door.

"Is everything all right?" she asked.

"I have never seen such good horses!" Perry replied. "Have a look if you get the chance! I have somehow to make the *Marquis* agree that they need exercising tomorrow morning!"

Kezia drew in her breath before she said:

"Do not forget to remind him you have . . . a wife who . . . loves riding!"

She moved towards the staircase, saying as she did so:

"Do not be late for dinner! Remember you have to serve

40

the wine. I have told Humber to do nothing more than bring in the dishes.''

''I will not forget,'' Perry promised, and walked towards the Drawing-Room as Kezia ran up the stairs.

When she reached her bedroom she thought that so far there had been no catastrophes, but she knew she was nervous about dinner.

She changed her clothes with lightning speed, finding that her mother's evening-gown fitted her and was, if she had time to look at herself, exceedingly becoming.

Clearly, it was not as fashionable as anything *Madame* de Salres would wear, but it made her skin look very white, and she put on the only piece of jewellery she possessed.

It was a narrow black velvet ribbon from which she had suspended a small pendant.

It was not expensive, but a pretty one, and as her neck was long, she thought the black velvet and the pendant made her look very dignified.

Now there was no time to think of her appearance, but only to concentrate on the dinner.

When she was dressed, she hurried to the kitchen to find out if there was anything she could do for Betsy.

To her relief, everything seemed to be in order.

She had prepared the first course during the afternoon and also the second, which was four small trout Perry had caught in the lake.

These she garnished with a French sauce and decorated with slices of lemon, which made the whole dish look very attractive.

The soup which preceded it was made of beetroot from the garden which grew without needing any attention.

Her mother had taught her how to make Borsch, which was a Russian dish.

As she added the thick cream to the heated soup she thought apprehensively of the very large bill they owed at the farm for all they had purchased for tonight's dinner.

When the soup was ready she ran quickly to the Drawing-Room and found to her relief that both the *Marquis* and *Madame* de Salres were there.

"Please do not think it unconventional," she said, "but as our Butler is very old and it is quite a long way to the Dining-Room, I am telling you that dinner is ready!"

The *Marquis* put down the glass he had in his hand.

"I am delighted to hear it!" he said.

Perry offered his arm to *Madame* de Salres.

"I 'ave not yet feeneeshed my champagne," she said.

Kezia felt she was saying it to be awkward.

"Then allow me to carry it in for you," Perry replied.

There was nothing *Madame* de Salres could do but put her hand on his arm as he picked up the glass, and they moved towards the Dining-Room.

As the *Marquis* reached Kezia, who was standing by the door, he said:

"I have an idea, Lady Falcon, that this is the first dinner party you have given since you have been married."

"Why should you think that?" Kezia asked.

"Because you are anxious for it to be a success and also a little apprehensive in case it is a failure."

Kezia laughed.

"I am only afraid because I feel that as you are so particular you will find our modest efforts at 'Haute Cuisine' do not compare with those in your own country."

"I will answer that after dinner," the *Marquis* said, "and I have a feeling and I am sure I am not wrong, that you know quite a lot about 'Haute Cuisine,' as you call it!"

Kezia looked at him in surprise.

It was true that her mother had taught her to make the French dishes which her father enjoyed.

As it happened, when they were first married they had spent quite a lot of time in France, but it would have been impossible for Betsy to tempt her father's palate.

Lady Falcon had therefore cooked the more difficult dishes for dinner, and Kezia had always helped her.

With new candles in the silver candelabra, which were the only light in the room, the table looked very glamorous.

Kezia had even found time to decorate the centre of the table with flowers.

Perry poured out the wine, and Old Humber came in with the plates of soup which, fortunately, were still hot.

Kezia was almost too frightened for the moment to eat.

The *Marquis* finished his plate and said:

"Delicious! I must congratulate you, Lady Falcon, on Course Number One!"

"You are making me nervous, *Monsieur*!" Kezia protested.

She knew as she spoke there would be nothing wrong with Course Number Two.

It was then that *Madame* de Salres decided to fascinate either the *Marquis* or Perry, Kezia was not sure which.

In a seductive voice she had not used previously, she flirted with both of them, holding each man completely captive so that there was no need for Kezia to speak.

Madame de Salres fluttered her eyelashes, which were mascaraed, and made every word she spoke seem to have a double meaning.

She was not actually beautiful.

But Kezia realised she was so fascinating that she could understand how Perry found it hard to keep his eyes off her.

She was not certain what the *Marquis* thought.

As she glanced at him and saw there was a twinkle in his eyes, she thought there was a sarcastic twist to his lips.

It was, Kezia thought towards the end of the meal, exactly like being on the stage.

They were all taking part in either a Comedy or a Drama in which the actors spoke witty, provocative words written for them by somebody else.

She was quite happy to listen and realise with satisfaction that the *Marquis* was enjoying the dinner.

The roasted baby lamb with its accompanying vegetables was a typically English dish.

She had made a cold *soufflé* exactly as her mother had taught her to do, which was very French and had a sauce which came from Paris.

There was no cheese, which Kezia knew was usually served at a French dinner.

Instead, she had provided an English savoury which was another of her father's favourites.

All Betsy had to do was to heat it up, and again the *Marquis* finished everything that was on his plate.

He also seemed to enjoy the claret which Perry had served with the lamb and a Sauterne which was poured out with the *soufflé*.

Madame de Salres was whispering something to Perry which she obviously did not wish anybody else to hear, and the *Marquis* said to Kezia:

"Now you can relax! And may I commend you, *Madame*, on the excellence of your meal, which was quite superlative and the equal, if not better, of anything I have eaten in Paris."

"That may not be true," Kezia said, "but it makes me very happy to hear you say it."

"How have you learnt to cook so well?" the *Marquis* asked. "And do not pretend that an English cook could have managed all these dishes, each of which had something to me very recognisable in it."

"My mother taught me," Kezia explained. "My parents spent a great deal of their time in France."

As she spoke she realised she was speaking as if she were herself, and added quickly:

"And I might say the same about my father and mother-in-law."

"I have always understood," the *Marquis* remarked, "that the English disapproved of cousins marrying."

Kezia knew he was thinking of the old adage that first cousins should never have children.

The idea made her shy, and she blushed as she said quickly:

"We are second cousins, and as we have known each other since we were children, it was perhaps natural that we should fall in love."

"And, of course, you are very, very much in love with your husband?"

He glanced as he spoke at Perry, who was captivated by *Madame* de Salres, who was saying something in a voice so low that neither he nor Kezia could hear her.

"Of course . . . I am!" Kezia replied firmly.

"And you have never been in love with anybody else?" the *Marquis* enquired.

"No . . . of course . . . not!"

Again she was speaking as herself, and added quickly:

"We have always been together."

"And yet your husband goes to London!" the *Marquis* said as if he were working it out. "I have seen him at several Race-Meetings without you."

"I have . . . so much to do . . . here," Kezia said.

"Then you do not mind him being away? Perhaps enjoying himself without you?"

Because she thought the *Marquis* was being far too inquisitive, Kezia said quickly:

"I think now *Madame* and I should leave you two gentlemen to your port."

She rose as she spoke, and for a moment *Madame* de Salres made no effort to leave the table.

Instead, once again she was whispering something in Perry's ear which made him laugh.

Then, as if she suddenly realised that Kezia had risen to her feet, she said:

"*Mon Dieu*! Always I forget this primitive custom of the Eengleesh of leaving the gentlemen at the table!"

She put out her hand and laid it on Perry's.

"Do not be long, *mon cher*," she said, "I so much prefer the conversation of men to the chitter-chatter of women!"

chapter three

KEZIA could not sleep.

She found herself going over and over everything in her mind and wondering if anything that would make their guests more comfortable had been forgotten.

She had remembered they would require drinking water in their bedrooms.

Fortunately two of the little glass jugs her mother had always loved had remained unbroken.

She had also remembered to put some Oil of White Violets for the bath in *Madame* de Salres' room. Her mother distilled it at the same time as her perfume.

Douglas had carried cans of water up to both rooms.

She had instructed him to empty and remove the baths afterwards and also to take away the bath-mats.

She had slipped upstairs before the others went to bed to make quite certain that their bedclothes were laid out.

She had been astonished at *Madame* de Salres' very transparent nightgown.

Although it was beautiful, she was sure her mother would have considered it very immodest.

At least dinner had been a success, and she could only pray that tomorrow night things would go off as smoothly.

She knew what a strain it was on Betsy to have to make extra meals for more people than usual, and in quick succession.

It was difficult to decide what she really thought of the *Marquis*.

He was so overwhelming and so much larger than she had expected, not only physically, but also mentally.

At the same time, she had to admit it had been interesting to talk to him.

He was certainly very different from what she had imagined a Frenchman would be like.

Then she remembered he had said when they were talking about the horses he had bought from the Duke:

"I am a Norman, and I always get what I want!"

A Norman!

Vaguely, at the back of her mind, she thought this meant something different from the fact that he just came from Normandy.

She lay thinking about it, then, as she had always done, she decided she must find out the right answer to her questions.

She got out of bed, put on the woollen dressing-gown she had worn for many years, and cautiously opened her door.

Everything was very quiet, and she knew her guests and Perry would be asleep.

She had deliberately left two sconces burning in the corridor.

She thought perhaps it would seem very dark and perhaps frightening if either of their guests came from their rooms.

There was no reason why they should do so, but the light made it easy for Kezia to go downstairs and along to the Library.

It was a large room, and the books were old, but she thought she knew exactly where to find every one of them.

It took her only a few seconds to put her hand on a copy of the *Encyclopaedia Britannica*.

When she wished to learn, she often thought how lucky she was that her grandfather, the ''Bad Baronet,'' had been so extravagant.

He had bought the *Encyclopaedia Britannica* when it was first published in 1758.

Now that the volumes had been added to it, the first edition looked very old and tattered.

The leather with which it was covered had lost its colour.

Kezia looked up Normandy, and under a brief description of the region she found what she was seeking.

Then, because it seemed so exciting, she gave an exclamation.

It had been the Vikings, Northmen or Normans, who had raided the coasts in the Emperor Charlemagne's time.

She read on, and found that the most important Norman Duke was Rollo, who was said to have died a pagan.

Even more fascinating was that his grandson became William the Conqueror—William I of England.

There was a great deal for Kezia to read.

The Normans first had been pagan destroyers bent on senseless plundering and slaughter, but as the centuries passed they became Knights.

They were still fierce, very strong, and over-powering.

Kezia felt that all these things applied to the *Marquis*.

It took her a long time to read, as there was a lot to say about the Normans.

In almost every country in which they settled they had become leaders and rulers, and in many ways, they were a law unto themselves.

They were so strong that a mere handful of Northmen could vanquish an enemy many times more numerous and had, she read, an unequalled capacity for rapid movement across land and sea.

But their great courage and their instinct, which made them victorious however unlikely the odds, turned them into supermen who it would have been impossible not to admire.

As she finished reading what had been written, Kezia gave a deep sigh.

She was always very moved by anything she read and felt in a way it became a part of herself.

Now she could not help thinking it was very exciting to have a Norman staying in the house.

The *Marquis* by his blood stood head and shoulders above other men.

She put the Encyclopaedia back on its shelf.

Then she blew out the candle, knowing she could find her way blindfolded back along the corridor into the hall and up the stairs.

She thought that tomorrow she would persuade the *Marquis* to talk to her about his ancestors.

She had read that Bayeux was one of the places in Normandy which had been annexed by Duke Rollo, and the Normans had settled there.

She reached the top of the stairs.

She was just about to walk along the corridor back to

her room when she was aware of a movement at the far end of it.

Instinctively, she stopped.

Then she realised in the very faint light coming from a candle still alight in its sconce, the door of *Madame* de Salres' bedroom had opened.

It flashed through Kezia's mind that perhaps, as Perry had suggested, she might be frightened.

In fact, earlier in the evening, when *Madame* de Salres had been talking to Perry, the *Marquis* had said to her:

"What are you worrying about? I can see an anxious look in your eyes."

Kezia had laughed.

"I am not worrying about anything now that you have enjoyed your dinner."

"I enjoyed it," the *Marquis* said, "and I ought to have thanked you for the flower arrangement on the table."

Kezia smiled.

"It was a pity that the only small flowers I could find were pansies."

"I have never seen them so well arranged," the *Marquis* said, "and I imagine you are also responsible for the flowers in this room, and, of course, in my bedroom."

"I am sorry there are so few water-lilies," Kezia said, "but they are only just coming into flower."

"I thought they were like you," the *Marquis* said quietly.

Kezia, however, did not realise that he had paid her a compliment.

Instead, she said:

"It was my . . . my . . . m—" she hesitated. "My mother-in-law who named all the bedrooms after flowers. I would like to have put *Madame* de Salres into the Rose Room so that I could decorate it with roses, but Perry thought she should be in the Lilac Room, and, of course, the lilac is over.''

''Why did your husband insist on that?'' the *Marquis* asked curiously.

''He said that she might be frightened or nervous in the night,'' Kezia explained, ''and therefore would want to be near to you.''

For a moment the *Marquis* looked surprised.

Then there was a faint smile on his lips which Kezia did not understand.

Now, as she saw him come from *Madame* de Salres' room, she thought perhaps she had called him and he had gone to her assistance.

Then, as he walked into his own room and shut the door, for the first time she understood why Perry had said it was insulting that he should bring *Madame* de Salres with him.

As the realisation of what he meant swept over her, she was so shocked that she was unable to move.

She could only stare along the corridor at the two doors side by side and think that she must be mistaken.

That could not have been the reason why the *Marquis* had gone to *Madame* de Salres' bedroom.

Then she told herself she was being very stupid.

Of course that was why Perry had been so insistent that she should go away.

That was why he had wanted to prevent her from meeting the *Marquis* just in case he should suggest to her that she should behave in the same manner as *Madame* de Salres.

''How could I . . . ever do . . . such a . . . thing?'' Kezia asked.

Now that the passage was empty, she ran as quickly as she could to her room and shut the door and locked it.

It was something she could never remember doing before.

But she felt as if she must barricade herself in so that not only the *Marquis*, but no other man could ever approach her in such a manner.

And yet, when she got into bed and thought it over, it seemed somehow part of the Norman character.

She remembered reading how the Vikings, when they invaded England had killed the men where they landed, ruined their crops and carried off their animals and their women.

She had wondered vaguely at the time why they had taken the women away and thought perhaps they used them as slaves.

Now she understood that they had a different reason for thrusting them into their longboats and taking them home.

She could imagine the *Marquis* doing the same thing, wearing a Viking helmet and looking fierce and frightening.

"Perry is right... he is a... bad man," she said to herself, "and the sooner he... buys the... necklace and... leaves the... better!"

She thought that if the necklace brought a curse upon him, it would be exactly what he deserved!

She wished his visit were over and she would never have to see him again.

*   *   *

In the morning everything seemed different.

When Perry found Kezia downstairs laying the table, he said:

"Your wish is granted, and you had better go upstairs and change!"

"What are you saying?" Kezia asked.

"The *Marquis* promised last night that we could ride with him immediately after breakfast."

Kezia gave a little gasp.

"Oh, Perry, did he really say we could ride his horses?"

"We have a choice of six," Perry said, "one of those ridden by the outriders won a gruelling Steeple-Chase last month, and I am astonished that the Duke agreed to part with him!"

Once again Kezia could hear the *Marquis* saying:

"I am a Norman, and I always get what I want!"

She was, however, not prepared to argue but just be grateful for the moment that she could ride a horse that was really outstanding.

Her riding-habit was worn, but the stiff lace-edged petticoat that went beneath it had been washed and starched.

So had the blouse of white muslin which was darned in several places.

Over it went a too tight-fitting jacket which gave her, although she was not aware of it, an extremely elegant figure.

She put on the small dark riding hat which did not disguise the red in her hair.

By the time the *Marquis* and Perry had finished their breakfast, Kezia was waiting for them outside the front door.

She was patting and longing to mount one of the three superb horses which the grooms had brought round from the stables.

Because of the shock of what she had learned the previous night, Kezia did not look at the *Marquis* as he came out into the sunshine to say:

"Good morning, Lady Falcon. I am glad you have decided to join your husband and me, and I hope my horse will not prove too obstreperous for you.''

Kezia guessed that because she was small and slight the *Marquis* thought she would not be able to control a spirited animal.

There was no use trying to explain that she had ridden since she could walk, so she merely said:

''Please, which horse may I ride?''

''I think you will find Thunderbolt, despite his name, the easiest,'' the *Marquis* replied.

Thunderbolt was a chestnut which Kezia had admired, and as she went eagerly to his side, the *Marquis* lifted her into the saddle.

For a moment, because he was touching her, she was conscious of a strange sensation she did not understand but which, she told herself, was repugnance.

She lifted the reins, and without waiting for the *Marquis* and Perry to mount the other horses started down the drive which led to the Park.

Thunderbolt was not tired after his journey of the previous day.

He expressed himself by bucking several times, then moving more quickly than Kezia wished him to.

She managed to keep him under control, and led the way through the Park, avoiding the low branches of the trees.

Then she was on the uncultivated ground where her father had always trained his horses.

It was also where she and Perry had galloped when they had horses to ride.

Now she had no intention of waiting for anybody.

She gave Thunderbolt his head, knowing as she did so that it was the most exciting thing that had happened to her for a very long time.

She must have ridden for nearly a mile before the *Marquis* and Perry caught up with her.

She thought her brother looked happier than she had seen him for a long time.

Now it was Perry's turn to lead the way, and they jumped several low hedges, then rode into a field where there was a much higher one.

The *Marquis*, looking ahead, frowned and said:

"I think, Lady Falcon, what lies ahead of us may be too much for you."

As she turned to answer, Kezia looked at him almost as if for the first time.

Never, she thought, had she seen a man look better on a horse, or so much a part of it.

That he was a superlative rider went without saying.

For the moment she could almost see him dressed in the heavy mail armour called hanbeck with a long broad-braided sword and a kite-shaped shield, bearing down upon his enemy.

"This is the most exciting thing I have done for years!" she replied. "So please, do not try to stop me!"

As she finished speaking, they had almost reached the jump, and as Thunderbolt took it with almost a foot to spare, she laughed with sheer delight.

Then they were galloping side by side, taking the next hedge they came to, and it was obvious the *Marquis* was no longer worried about her.

Only when they turned for home was Kezia able to say:

"Thank you . . . thank you! I do not remember when I have . . . ever been so . . . happy!"

"I was just about to say the same thing," Perry agreed, "and I only wish I could afford horses the equal of these!"

"I expect they are available if you look for them," the

Marquis replied, "and I consider those in my stables at home are better!"

"Now you are boasting!" Kezia said, "for I do not believe any horse could be better than Thunderbolt!"

"Then I see that is something I shall have to prove to you," the *Marquis* answered, "but we will talk about that later."

She wondered what he meant, and told herself she really had no desire to talk to him.

He had shocked her, and Perry had been right in saying he was the type of man she should not meet.

At the same time, she had to admit that his horses and, if she were honest, the man himself, had brought something new and exciting into her life.

When he was gone and she was alone again, she thought about how she would dream that she was riding Thunderbolt.

She would also, although she would try not to, repeat in her mind everything the *Marquis* had said.

'He is a Norman, and Normans are pagans!' she thought despairingly.

She glanced at him and thought it was impossible for any man to look so regal, so undoubtedly a conqueror.

"Your land needs cultivating!" the *Marquis* said to Perry unexpectedly.

"I realise that," Perry replied, "but for the moment I cannot afford to farm it."

"Are you really so poor?" the *Marquis* asked. "Your walls hold a great many fine pictures which are undoubtedly valuable."

"Find me one that is not entailed," Perry replied, "and I will be happy to sell it to you!"

"I apologise," the *Marquis* exclaimed. "That was stupid

of me! I had forgotten that the English entail everything onto their eldest son!"

There was silence for some minutes, then the *Marquis* said:

"At least I understand the necklace I have come to see is saleable."

"Which, I assure you, is very fortunate for me!" Perry answered.

"Then we will look at it this afternoon," the *Marquis* said, "and if you are not tired of riding, we can exercise my other three horses after luncheon."

Kezia gave a cry of delight.

"Oh, please," she begged, "do let us do that! When you leave tomorrow I shall have only poor old Dobbin to ride, and he is so slow that I can go more quickly on my own two feet."

The *Marquis* laughed.

"That is certainly a very sad story, and I am sure it is something your husband will be able to rectify."

Kezia knew he was referring to the sale of the necklace, and she said:

"Perry wants me to go to London to attend the Balls and be presented to the Queen, but if I could have a horse like this one, I would much rather stay here and ride!"

"Then that is something you will have to wish for very hard," the *Marquis* said, "as I am sure you know, it is only by our own will-power that wishes come true!"

"That is what I want to believe," Kezia said, "but sometimes it is . . . difficult."

Then without thinking she added:

"It is easy for you because you are a Norman, and Normans have always been conquerors."

The *Marquis* looked amused.

"So you think that is what I am?"

"It is certainly in your blood."

"How do you know this?"

"I have been reading about the Normans in the Encyclopaedia," Kezia said truthfully.

"Were you interested in me, or the Normans?" the *Marquis* asked.

She looked at him, and there was an expression in his eyes that made her look away again.

She remembered what she had found out last night when she was returning from the Library.

Without answering the question she just touched Thunderbolt with her whip, then was galloping away.

It was some time before the two men caught up with her.

Luncheon was to be a light meal in order to save Betsy for the effort she would have to make preparing dinner.

Kezia hurried to the kitchen as soon as they got back to the house.

She made the salad dressing and finished off the first course, which Betsy had started.

She added butter to the vegetables, which had been forgotten, then found she had no time to change her clothes.

She had taken off her riding-hat and jacket and now she went into the Dining-Room wearing her white muslin blouse and riding-skirt.

She looked very young and, as it happened, very lovely, but she avoided the *Marquis*' eyes and said good-morning to *Madame* de Salres.

The contrast between her and the Frenchwoman was, Kezia thought, almost ludicrous.

Madame de Salres, who had only just come from her bedroom, was wearing a gown which had the voluminous skirt that had just come into fashion.

The pleating on the hem, the lace, the little touches of velvet, were all part of the genius of a French Couturier.

Madame de Salres looked as if she had just stepped out of a picture-frame.

She regarded Kezia first in surprise, then with a disdain which made her feel very small and insignificant.

Then as if she was of no consequence, *Madame* flirted, as she had last night, both with the *Marquis* and with Perry.

She had an expertise that was unmistakably French.

Kezia made no effort to join in the conversation.

She knew there was a great deal of it she did not understand, and the rest she did not want to.

She was vividly aware now that *Madame* de Salres was what the servants would call "a scarlet woman."

She thought her ancestors in their frames on the wall were looking down with disapproval.

She became suddenly aware that the *Marquis* was looking at her and she had the frightening feeling that he could read her thoughts.

Quickly she said:

"You have not told us, *Monsieur*, about your *Château* in Normandy. Is it a Norman Castle?"

"I am afraid not," the *Marquis* replied. "There was a Castle several centuries ago, but it has been replaced by the *Château* which I think you will admire when you see it."

That was something which was very unlikely, Kezia thought.

With an effort she said:

"My mother and father have . . . told me about the *Château* of France and how beautiful they were before the Revolution. I believe, however, Normandy did not suffer any great damage."

"Certainly not as bad as in the centre of France," the *Marquis* said, "and of course near Paris."

"You were lucky."

"I like to think I am," he replied, "and very lucky in coming here."

Again there was that expression in his eyes that made her feel shy, and she said quickly:

"As you have finished luncheon, I think I will get ready to go riding so that I shall not keep you waiting."

"Rideeng?" *Madame* de Salres exclaimed. "You cannot mean you are going rideeng again? *Tiens*, Vere, 'ow can you be so ungallant and so unkind?"

"There are three horses for us to exercise," the *Marquis* remarked.

"'Orses! 'Orses!" *Madame* de Salres exclaimed. "We poor women will 'ave to grow four legs if we are to compete!"

"I can only say, *Madame*," Perry said, "that you manage very skilfully to eclipse everybody and everything with two!"

Madame de Salres smiled at him.

"*Merci, mon brave!* You are very kind and very encouraging, which is more than can be said for *Monsieur le Marquis!*"

She threw a provocative glance at the *Marquis* as if she were challenging him.

There was, however, a twist to the *Marquis*' lips as he replied:

"You know, Yvonne, you do not enjoy riding, and therefore we look to you to entertain our hearts and our minds when we have exercised our bodies."

"I can theenk of other ways for you to do that!" *Madame* de Salres said.

The way she spoke made even Kezia understand what she meant.

She rose from the table quickly, saying in a voice that sounded loud and sharp even to herself:

"As luncheon is over, I think you would be more comfortable in the Drawing-Room!"

She walked to the door and before the *Marquis* could open it for her, she had left the room and was moving quickly down the passage.

She felt that *Madame* de Salres was, with her innuendoes, making her feel dirty.

"I hate her!" she told herself as she went up the stairs.

Then, as she reached her bedroom, she remembered that the *Marquis* had not yet seen the necklace.

If it was for *Madame* de Salres and she disparaged it, then perhaps he would not buy it.

"Help me . . . Mama . . . not to be . . . stupid over . . . this," she prayed, "but it does . . . seem wrong . . . and is spoiling . . . everything you . . . made so . . . beautiful."

She knew as she put on her jacket and her hat that it might be the sensible thing not to accompany the *Marquis* and Perry.

But the temptation of riding the *Marquis'* horses was too strong for her to resist.

When she went downstairs she found to her surprise that only the *Marquis* was waiting for her in the hall.

"Where is Perry?" she asked.

"Your husband is playing the perfect host," the *Marquis* replied, "and as *Madame* de Salres does not wish to be left alone, he is taking her driving in his Phaeton."

Kezia gave a little cry of horror.

"He should not do that! He so enjoys riding your horses, and he may never have the chance to do so again."

"I promise he shall have the chance."

"But . . . how?" Kezia asked bluntly.

"I will answer that a little later," the *Marquis* said, "and perhaps what you are really objecting to is that he is escorting *Madame* de Salres."

Without thinking Kezia replied:

"Oh, no, not if it amuses him! But I feel sure he would rather be riding."

As she spoke she thought there was no point in arguing about it and Perry would do as he wanted.

She therefore walked out through the front door and did not see the expression in the *Marquis'* eyes.

Having mounted their horses, they went the same way as they had gone in the morning.

Only when they had taken the higher fences and slowed their horses down to a walk did the *Marquis* say:

"I have seen many women ride, but I think without exception you are better than any of them!"

"If you are speaking the truth," Kezia replied, "then it is the most wonderful compliment I have ever been paid!"

"I find that hard to believe," the *Marquis* said, "just as when you said this morning that it was the happiest time you have ever spent, it could not have been true!"

"It is true!" Kezia said in a rapt little voice. "I never thought I would ever ride such a wonderful horse, or jump high hedges with so little difficulty."

"I would have expected the happiest time of your life would have been your wedding day!"

Too late Kezia thought she had been over-enthusiastic.

"That . . . is something . . . different," she said a little lamely after a pause.

"In what way?" the *Marquis* asked.

Kezia could not think of a suitable reply, and after a moment he said:

"You puzzle and bewilder me, and at the same time, I find you very intriguing!"

Because what he said was so surprising, Kezia turned to look at him and found once again the expression in his blue eyes made her feel shy.

"I think we . . . should be . . . going back," she said.

"You cannot always run away," the *Marquis* remarked.

"Who says I am doing that?"

"It is what you are doing," he answered, "and it is something I want to prevent."

"I cannot think why."

"As I have said, you intrigue me," the *Marquis* answered, "you are very different from any Englishwoman I have ever known, just as your undeniable beauty is different."

"I am sure that is . . . something you have . . . said to a . . . hundred women!" Kezia said lightly.

The *Marquis* frowned.

"You are well aware that I am speaking the truth. Just as I can read your thoughts, you can read mine, and you know I am not flattering you!"

Kezia looked at him in astonishment, and for several moments her eyes were held by his.

Now she could read his thoughts, and knew that they were somehow speaking to each other without words.

Then she said:

"Please . . . Perry . . . warned me about you . . . and now you are . . . frightening me!"

"Because I am not what you expected?" the *Marquis* asked.

"I think it is . . . because you are a . . . Norman . . . and

I have . . . never met anybody like you . . . also because . . . if you think I am different . . . you are . . . very, very different!''

"You are different,'' the *Marquis* said quietly, "because I understand exactly what you are saying, just as you also understand without there being any need for explanations.''

"B-but . . . there is . . . there must be!'' Kezia said. "And it is a . . . mistake for us to . . . talk like . . . this.''

"What you are really thinking,'' the *Marquis* replied, "is that you are frightened because we think alike, and it is quite comprehensible to us both.''

It was not what he said, but the depth of his voice.

Yet she knew he was speaking sincerely, and there was nothing flirtatious behind his words.

Because she was suddenly at a loss, and also afraid of her own feelings, Kezia ran away.

She rode home as quickly as she could, aware that the *Marquis* was beside her, and yet she neither looked at him nor spoke.

His servants were waiting for them outside the front door.

As she brought her horse to a standstill, Kezia slipped down from the saddle and, without waiting for the *Marquis* ran up the steps and into the hall.

The stairs were in front of her.

Before she could reach them the *Marquis* caught hold of her arm and turned her round to face him.

"Why should you run away?'' he asked in his deep voice.

"I have . . . already given . . . you the . . . answer to . . . that!''

"That you are frightened? But why? Think of it not as something physically frightening, but as if we have suddenly reached the top of the mountain, or crossed a desert towards the horizon only to find there is another beyond it.''

65

Now he had a hand on each of Kezia's shoulders, and it was impossible for her to move.

She felt as if he were hypnotising her by what he was saying, and she was also tinglingly aware that he was touching her.

For a long moment he looked at her. Then he said:

"Run, and go on running! But, remember, as a Norman, I shall catch you, and there is no escape!"

Then, as she stared at him, understanding what he was saying, but at the same time trying not to, he turned and walked away.

With a superhuman effort Kezia ran up the stairs towards her bedroom.

* * *

Perry did not say anything when he came back from his drive with *Madame* de Salres.

Nor did he seem to mind having missed the chance of riding one of the *Marquis'* horses.

Instead, he looked rather pleased with himself, Kezia thought.

However, *Madame* de Salres looked at the *Marquis* defiantly, as if she had scored a point off him.

They had gone into the Drawing-Room at four o'clock for an English tea.

Kezia thought it was one way of keeping them entertained whether they wanted to drink it or not.

The *Marquis*, however, ate the cucumber sandwiches and said he enjoyed them, while *Madame* de Salres sipped a little tea and made a grimace.

Perry ate as if he was hungry, and Kezia knew he was

really waiting for the moment when he would fetch the necklace.

Finally the *Marquis* finished his cup of tea and said:

"Now, Falcon, where is this treasure you promised to show us? And I am sure Yvonne wants to hear the story of how the *Comtesse* de la Motte managed to cause the greatest scandal France has ever known."

"*Tiens*! I 'ave 'eard eet before," *Madame* de Salres remarked, "and I 'ave always thought 'ow fooleesh she was to be found out!"

The *Marquis* laughed.

"That, of course, is the Eleventh Commandment: '*Thou shalt not be found out!*' and those who break it must undoubtedly pay the penalty!"

"At least she managed to salvage sometheeng from the wreckage," *Madame* de Salres went on, "so let us see ze necklace, and find out if, after all 'er intriguing, eet was worth while."

"I am sure it was not!" Kezia said. "She was taken to prison, and having escaped to London, she could never return to her native land, so she died in exile."

"I am sure she must 'ave consoled 'erself weeth some 'andsome Engleeshman," *Madame* de Salres laughed.

She looked at Perry as she spoke, and there was no doubt he found her very alluring, and the expression in his eyes was very obvious.

Kezia did not seem concerned, and after a moment the *Marquis* asked:

"Well, where is the necklace? We are all waiting."

Perry got quickly to his feet.

"I will go to fetch it."

He went to his bedroom, where Kezia knew he kept the

67

necklace hidden in a secret place known only to the reigning Baronet.

Actually she knew it, too, because Perry had shown her where it was, so that if necessary she could move the necklace somewhere else when he was away.

Now, as they waited in the Drawing-Room, *Madame* de Salres threw out her long-fingered hands towards the *Marquis* as she said:

" 'Ave you missed me, my charming, unpredictable *cher ami*?"

"But of course!" the *Marquis* replied without taking her hand.

"Then perhaps, if you ask me very nicely, I will forgive you for being so unkind to me last night."

She spoke in French, as if she thought Kezia would not understand, and the *Marquis* replied in the same language:

"I think it is something we should discuss when we are alone."

Madame de Salres gave a little laugh.

"You do not imagine these English who are so insular that they never learn another language can understand?" she queried. "But as you say, when we are alone I will pardon you for what you did not do while I would much prefer to show my gratitude for what you did!"

It was now very obvious to Kezia what she was saying.

Quite suddenly, because she knew that the *Marquis* had not made love to *Madame* de Salres the night before, she felt unexpectedly happy.

The sun coming through the window was brilliant, and she thought she could hear the birds singing.

Then she asked herself how it was possible she could understand.

Yet whether she was reading the *Marquis*' thoughts or

not, she knew that last night, while he had gone to say goodnight to *Madame* de Salres, he had not made love to her.

Because Kezia was very innocent and had lived such a quiet life, she had no idea what a man did when he made love to a woman.

She knew that something happened which could be very wonderful.

At the same time, without love it would also be primitive, frightening, and even revolting.

She was aware that Royalty made arranged marriages, as well as the aristocratic families of England, and, of course, in France.

Because her father and mother had married for love, she had always imagined it was something which would happen to her one day.

Somehow, although it was difficult to think how, she would meet the man of her dreams.

To marry for money or for position was something so unthinkable that it never occurred to her.

What she could not understand was why men pursued women they had no wish to marry.

They apparently made love to them even though they could never mean anything important in their lives.

It was a subject on which she had not wasted much thought because it seemed so incomprehensible.

Yet last night when she had been shocked by the *Marquis* coming from *Madame* de Salres' bedroom, she had felt a revulsion against anything that was so wrong.

It was, although she could not quite understand it, so ugly.

Now she knew why *Madame* de Salres had been flirting with Perry. Maybe, as she had said herself, she was punishing the *Marquis* for what he had *not* done last night.

Kezia had no idea how expressive her face was as she thought over what had just been said.

Then Perry came back into the room.

He was carrying in his hand a large leather box.

As he reached the *Marquis* he lifted the lid, then handed it to him.

Lying on black velvet was the famous necklace made of twenty-one large diamonds which had been stolen from the huge necklace intended for Queen Marie-Antoinette.

As the stones flashed and shone in the sunshine they seemed dazzling.

For a moment there was complete silence until *Madame* de Salres said, her voice full of greed:

"Eet ees beautiful! *Magnifique!* Oh, Vere, *Mon Cher*, my marvellous lover, give eet to me!"

Her voice seemed to break the spell which had held the *Marquis* silent.

Then he looked at the Frenchwoman with a hardness in his eyes which made him, Kezia thought, seem more overwhelming and frightening than he had ever been before.

Slowly, he closed the lid of the box.

"No," he said, and he seemed almost to drawl the words. "No, this is not for you!"

chapter four

FOR a moment there was complete silence.

Then *Madame* de Salres gave a shrill scream.

" 'Ow can you be so unkind, so 'eartless?" she asked, her words tumbling over themselves. "I geeve you my love, my 'eart, and you will not even geeve to me thees necklace!"

The *Marquis* did not reply and, as if overcome by her feelings, she swept out of the room, still screaming as she did so of his cruelty and unkindness.

As she went she left three people staring after her in astonishment.

Then the *Marquis* said in a quiet tone:

"I am certainly prepared, Falcon, to buy this necklace from you, but on one condition."

Kezia felt her heart almost miss a beat.

She was sure the *Marquis* was going to say that it was too expensive, in which case perhaps Perry would refuse to sell the necklace, hoping for another purchaser.

If that happened, how could they possibly pay the bills they owed, or continue to live in the house?

"Condition?" Perry questioned.

There was no doubt that he, too, was perturbed, but the *Marquis* had opened the leather box again and was looking at the necklace.

"I want this," he said, "for a Museum on my estate which will contain mementos of the Revolution."

He paused before he went on:

"That of course includes furniture and pictures of the reign of Louis XV."

Kezia was listening intently, but she was still holding her breath.

"Of course this necklace is a very important exhibit," the *Marquis* said, "and I will pay the sum you are asking for it."

With difficulty Kezia stifled a cry of delight.

She knew without even looking at him that Perry, who had been very tense, was now relaxed.

"What is the condition?" he asked after a long pause.

"Because I wish to have the setting altered," the *Marquis* explained, "in order to make it a little more impressive than it is at present, I cannot take it with me when I return to France next week. Instead, I want you and your wife to bring it with you when you come to stay with me, on the tenth of June."

"The tenth of June?" Perry repeated almost stupidly.

The *Marquis* smiled.

"I am arranging a Race-Meeting in which I know you would like to participate, and I also thought, as these new horses jump so well, that I would also organise a Steeple-Chase."

Perry's whole face seemed to light up.

Then, as Kezia made a little sound, he suddenly remembered her.

"It is something I should enjoy enormously," he said. "At the same time, I think it will be impossible for Kezia to accompany me, as I know she has commitments here which will prevent her from leaving."

The *Marquis* snapped the leather case shut and put it down on the small table beside the chair in which Perry was sitting.

"In which case," he said, "and of course I understand how busy your wife is, I will however have to deny myself the pleasure of adding the necklace to my Collection."

He rose to his feet as he spoke and started to walk towards the door.

Perry looked frantically at Kezia, whose face had gone very pale.

For a moment her voice seemed to have died in her throat, then, when the *Marquis* had almost reached the door, she said:

"Wait . . . please . . . wait! I do have . . . as Perry has said . . . some previous engagements . . . but I am . . . sure I can . . . cancel them!"

Her words seemed to tumble over themselves, and slowly the *Marquis* turned back.

"You are—quite sure you can do that?" he asked.

"Quite . . . q-quite . . . s-sure," she stammered.

Then, as her eyes met his, she knew he had been certain from the very beginning of the conversation that he would get his own way.

Once again he was the victor, the conqueror, a Norman who was never defeated.

*   *   *

Because she felt almost exhausted by the drama of what had happened, Kezia went up to her bedroom.

Sitting down in a chair by the window, she put her hands over her face.

They had won!

They had obtained the fortune Perry had asked for the necklace, but at the same time everything seemed more complicated than it had been when the *Marquis* had first arrived.

How could she possibly go to France and stay in the *Marquis' Château* pretending to be Perry's wife?

What was she to do at the moment about *Madame* de Salres, who, shut in her bedroom, was still hysterical?

She tried to tell herself that nothing mattered except that the dark cloud of debts and despair had been lifted from over their heads.

Now she could do all the things that had been left undone, and a great many more besides.

'First we must pay Humber and Betsy their wages which are so long overdue,' Kezia thought. ''Secondly we must repair the cottages for the pensioners, help the farmers, and put into cultivation the fields nearest to the house.''

Then she thought of the roof, the windows, the stove in the kitchen.

There were a thousand other things before she remembered that now she would be able to afford to buy a horse.

She got to her feet to look out of the window.

As she did so she thought she could already see the garden tidy, and looking as it had when she was a child.

The door of her bedroom suddenly opened, and as she turned Perry came into the room.

"I have it!" he said triumphantly, waving a cheque in his hand.

He walked across to her, put his arms around her shoulders, and hugged her.

"We are rich!" he said. "Rich, Kezia, and it is all due to you! I am sure if the *Marquis* had not enjoyed himself so much, he would have gone away without the necklace."

"But . . . we have to . . . take it to . . . him," Kezia said in a low voice.

"I know that," Perry replied, "but I would take it down into Hell rather than lose the sale. I was only trying to do what was best for you."

"I realised that," Kezia said, "and it will be very . . . embarrassing to have to . . . pretend when we are . . . in France that we are . . . married."

"We will not stay long," Perry said reassuringly. "The Race will take place the day after we arrive and we can leave the day after it is over."

Kezia wanted to say that there was so much to see that having got to France it would be a pity to leave too quickly.

But she thought it unwise to argue about it with Perry at this particular moment.

"I shall have to . . . have some . . . new clothes," she said, "although I may be able to . . . alter one or . . . two of Mama's gowns."

"You shall have the gowns you have been owed for a long time," Perry promised.

"Thank you very much, Dearest," Kezia said. "But remember, the money will not . . . last for . . . ever!"

She hesitated, then she added:

"Please, Perry do . . . not . . . gamble with any of it!"

"I am not such a fool as that," he answered, "and I do not intend to go to London until after we come back from France. There is a great deal here for me to do."

Kezia pushed away her doubts and thought she must be enthusiastic and happy as her brother was.

Perry was looking at the cheque he held in his hand as if he could hardly believe it was real.

Then he said:

"Oh, by the way, I had forgotten, but the *Marquis* thought there was still time before dinner for you to show him the house. He particularly wanted to see the rooms because I told him the four-poster in which I sleep came originally from Cornwall, and apparently, he is interested in the carving."

"I expect he is comparing it with what the craftsmen produced in Normandy," Kezia said. "Where is he?"

"I left him in the Library, where he went to write this cheque," Perry said.

He looked at it again, and added:

"We really ought to frame this and exhibit it in the same way as the *Marquis* will show the necklace!"

Kezia laughed.

"Put it quickly in the bank so that we can draw out the money as we need it, otherwise it may fly away and you will find you only imagined it!"

"Do not say anything so terrible," Perry said in mock horror, "and go now and do what the *Marquis* wants."

He paused for a moment. Then he said, almost as if he spoke to himself:

"I wonder if I ought to try to placate Yvonne?"

Kezia looked at him in surprise.

"No, of course not!" she said. "She is in her bedroom!"

Perry hesitated. Then he said:

"That is right, and I expect she will recover when the *Marquis* gives her more diamonds to add to the collection she has already."

Kezia looked at Perry wide-eyed.

"Are you saying that the *Marquis* gave her all those wonderful jewels she has been wearing while she has been here?"

"I expect so," Perry said. "Rich men always have to pay heavily for their amusements."

Once again Kezia was shocked.

It seemed incredible that anyone would spend so much on one woman for what Perry called "amusement."

Because it was something she did not wish to discuss with her brother, she walked towards the door, saying:

"I will show the *Marquis* the four-poster. I hope your room is tidy!"

"I doubt it," Perry replied.

Kezia went downstairs to the Library and found the *Marquis* with the Encyclopaedia in his hand.

He looked up as she approached him and said with an amused note in his voice:

"Now I see what you have been reading about me! Do you really think I am a primitive pagan, ruthless and over-powering?"

"You have not read far enough," Kezia replied. "You forget the Normans, having started like that, became Knights."

"But they were still conquerors."

"Of course . . . as undoubtedly you . . . are!"

"I wonder," he said. "Perhaps some things are unobtainable."

"That does not sound like a Norman speaking," Kezia said teasingly. "I am sure they were never faint-hearted when they went into battle, but completely and absolutely certain they would be victorious."

"So that is what you want me to be?" the *Marquis* asked.

He was looking at her, and suddenly she thought there might be an innuendo in what they had been saying to each other.

Quickly, because she thought he might know what she was thinking, she said:

"I want you to fight for what is right and what is good, and what will . . . help other . . . people."

"And what about ourselves?"

"What could give you more satisfaction than knowing you are battling against evil?"

"It depends on what you call evil," the *Marquis* said quietly.

Kezia had the idea that they were duelling with words.

Once again she could see him in his chain-mail armour, his shield in one hand, a light spear in the other.

She could see him so vividly that she was not surprised when the *Marquis* said:

"That is a fanciful picture you are looking at! I am also a man, Kezia!"

She gave a little laugh because it seemed so ridiculous that he could understand her thoughts.

Then she replied:

"A man, but a Norman, and much more is therefore expected of you."

Then before the *Marquis* could reply, and because she had the feeling she was moving on dangerous ground, she said:

"Perry said you . . . wanted to see the bed in which . . . his ancestors have slept since before the time of William the Conqueror's invasion of England."

"It is really possible it could last so long?" the *Marquis* asked in a very different voice from what he had used before.

"I think perhaps its age has been exaggerated," Kezia admitted, "but it is very old, so come and look at it."

They walked up the stairs side by side, and it struck her they might be climbing the mountain to which he had referred before.

"That would be harder!" he said.

Kezia laughed.

"If you keep reading my thoughts, there will be no need for me to say anything and we can just sit in silence."

"As long as I am with you," the *Marquis* said, "it does not really matter what we do."

The way he spoke made Kezia feel as if her heart turned a somersault.

She hurried along the corridor in which the bedrooms they all slept were.

At the far end of it there was the room which had been the Master's ever since the house had been built.

It was larger than all the other State-Bedrooms, and there were three diamond-paned windows in it, besides a large open fireplace in which it was possible to burn half a tree.

The beams of the ceiling were carved, and two of the walls were panelled.

But it was impossible to look at anything but the huge four-poster.

It was of oak and carved with animals, people, and ships—all things familiar to the ancient craftsmen.

It was not very high, but wide and surmounting the front of it was the Falcon crest with its Latin motto carved beneath it.

Kezia's mother had added new curtains of crimson velvet

and had embroidered a velvet bed-cover with the Falcon coat-of-arms.

She had done it skilfully, and it had taken her nearly two years to complete.

While the rest of the room was somewhat shabby, the bed-cover and the curtains seemed to glow, almost as if a special light made them do so.

The *Marquis* stood looking at it for a long time before he said:

"It is different in every way from anything I have seen before, and I have a great deal of carving to show you when you come to my *Château*."

"I loved this when I was a child," Kezia said, "and I used to look for the ducks as well as the rabbits and the squirrels which you can find peeping from between the trees."

"So you were here as a child!"

Kezia started, then remembered she had been speaking as herself.

"Yes, of course," she said quickly. "I often came to stay with my parents."

Because she was lying, she looked away from the *Marquis*, afraid that his intuition where she was concerned would tell him that she was not speaking the truth.

He looked around the room. Then he said:

"It is a very masculine room, and there appears to be no trace of you in it, which I would have expected to find."

Kezia thought quickly.

"I sleep in a different room," she said, "because Perry snores, and also, because I am here alone so much, I find my own room more cozy and perhaps with not so many ghosts in it!"

"I would like to see your room," the *Marquis* said.

Kezia thought it was a mistake, but she could think of no reason for refusing.

She walked towards the door, saying:

"First I would like to show you the other rooms."

She opened the door of the room next to Perry's and said:

"This was my . . . my mother-in-law's room."

Even as she entered it, she wondered why she had taken the *Marquis*, of all people, into the room she had always thought of as a special shrine to her mother.

It was too late now to go back.

She pulled aside the curtains so that he could see a very different bed from the one they had been looking at in the Master's Bedroom.

This was a four-poster, too, and it was also carved, but it was gilded and the posts had a very delicate design.

At the top of the bed were small cupids carrying garlands of flowers.

The *Marquis* looked at it in silence, until at last he said:

"This is a room of love, and I find it strange that you do not sleep in it!"

"I left it as it was when my . . . mother-in-law was alive," Kezia replied.

She moved quickly from the room, and there was nothing the *Marquis* could do but follow her.

She showed him the Rose Room, then she came to her own.

As she put out her hand towards the door she hesitated, saying:

"I am sure it will soon be time for us to dress for dinner."

"I have not yet seen your room," the *Marquis* objected.

He spoke quietly, but Kezia felt a force behind the words that commanded her to do what he wished.

Because he somehow made her feel helpless, she opened the door and he saw the room she had slept in ever since she was a child.

The bed was not elaborate, or carved, as in the other rooms.

It was draped in white muslin and the curtains fell from a small corolla, almost like a halo, which was attached to the ceiling.

Her dressing-table also had what the servants called "*a muslin petticoat*," and the curtains were draped with a frill.

They were caught back on each side of the window with a rope covered in silk flowers.

It was a very lovely room.

Because she was so much alone and spent more time in it than anywhere else in the house, Kezia had moved the pictures she liked best to hang on the walls.

Now she realised for the first time that they were all French.

She had chosen them because they had some spiritual meaning for her that was difficult to put into words.

As the *Marquis* looked at them she knew he understood, and waited to hear what he had to say.

She thought he would never speak, then when he did he said quietly:

"I would have known this was your room even if I had come here alone!"

With that he walked to the door, opened it, passed through, and shut it behind him, leaving Kezia inside.

*   *   *

As she dressed for dinner, Kezia felt apprehensive in case *Madame* de Salres continued to make a scene about the necklace.

But when she came down, the Frenchwoman was all smiles and charm.

She flirted with Perry, and at the same time she was polite and more pleasant to Kezia than she had been since she had first arrived.

Kezia felt certain it was something the *Marquis* had said to her or done.

Whatever it was, she was grateful there were to be no more dramatic demands for the necklace while she and Perry were present.

Dinner was not as good as it had been the previous night.

This was due, Kezia thought guiltily, to the fact that she had not spent as much time in the kitchen as she should have done.

But at least it was edible, and no-one complained.

Because Perry was in such a good humour, they all seemed to be laughing and enjoying themselves.

Madame de Salres held the table by fascinating both the men with an expertise which Kezia did not even attempt to emulate.

Then later they were in the Drawing-Room. *Madame* de Salres and Perry walked through the French windows into the Rose-Garden.

This left Kezia alone with the *Marquis*.

Because it was uppermost in her mind, she said:

"I want to thank you for buying the . . . diamond necklace. It will make all the difference to Perry . . . and a great number of . . . other people. Since they are unable to thank you themselves . . . I will do it for them."

"And that will make you happy?" the *Marquis* enquired.

"Very . . . very happy," Kezia said. "It has become more and more difficult to keep . . . things going . . . wondering . . . where the next . . . penny is to . . . come from."

"But your husband goes to London," the *Marquis* said reflectively, "and enjoys a social life which most people find very expensive."

"Perry is asked for himself . . . and does not have to . . . extend hospitality," Kezia said a little lamely.

"While you are content to stay here?"

"I shall be content," Kezia replied, "now that you have so . . . generously bought . . . the necklace."

"I would like to be even more generous," the *Marquis* said, "but I feel it is something you will not allow me to be."

Kezia looked up at him in surprise, and he saw by her expression that she did not understand.

"When you come to France," he said, "I wish to give you one of my horses, and you will have quite a number to choose from."

For a moment the expression on Kezia's face was dazzling, then she said:

"No . . . no . . . of course . . . not! It is . . . something I cannot . . . accept."

"Why not?"

"Because it . . . would be . . . incorrect."

"And you think your husband might be jealous?"

"No . . . not . . . jealous," Kezia said without thinking, "but envious."

"Then of course," the *Marquis* said, "I shall have to give him one too."

"No . . . no," Kezia replied. "I did not mean that . . . of

course I did . . . not mean that! In any case you have given us . . . quite enough . . . already and we could not possibly . . . presume on you for . . . anything else."

She thought as she spoke how shocked her mother would have been at the idea of any man giving her such an expensive present as a horse.

Before the *Marquis* could speak she said:

"Please . . . forget you made . . . such a suggestion . . . for I am sure your horses . . . who are French . . . would be much . . . happier in their own . . . country . . . than in an alien land."

"As a Norman," the *Marquis* said, "I consider myself partly English, and as a conquered person, as you say your ancestors were at the Battle of Hastings, I think you will have to obey me, and do as I tell you to do."

Kezia laughed.

"Nobody would think that was a very logical argument."

"It is logical enough for me to insist that you choose a horse amongst those in my stables, but we will talk about it when you come to the *Château* Bayeux, and I can return your hospitality, which I have enjoyed more than I can possibly say."

Because of the way he spoke, the very air seemed to be vibrating round them.

Because she suddenly felt nervous, Kezia said:

"I do hope *Madame* de Salres does not catch cold. Even though it is Summer, there can still be a chill wind in the evening."

"I assure you Yvonne can look after herself, as she has already managed to do," the *Marquis* said cynically, "and your husband will undoubtedly prevent her from feeling chilled!"

Now there was a definite note in his voice which made

Kezia feel he was annoyed with Perry, and she said quickly:

"Perry always . . . tries to be the . . . perfect host, and *Madame* is very, very attractive!"

"When I brought her here," the *Marquis* said, "I had no idea that Sir Peregrine was married, and I was aware the moment I saw you that I had made a mistake."

Because he was apologising, Kezia felt embarrassed.

"Please do not . . . think like that," she said. "*Madame* is so beautiful, so fascinating, and so elegantly dressed . . . I know how different I look, and you . . . must find it . . . very boring."

"Do you really think anything we have said or done since I have been here could possibly be described as boring?" the *Marquis* asked.

Now there was a deep note in his voice that seemed to vibrate through Kezia in a strange way.

"I am . . . expressing myself . . . very badly," she replied, "but I think . . . you understand."

"I do understand," the *Marquis* answered, "but I do not know quite what I can do about it, and God knows, that is something I have never said before in my whole life."

Kezia looked at him in surprise.

Then when she was about to ask him for an explanation, *Madame* de Salres and Perry returned from the garden.

Eagerly, as if she were a young girl, the Frenchwoman ran across to the *Marquis*.

She almost threw herself against him as she said in French:

"It is so romantic outside in the moonlight, and under the stars. Come and look at them with me, Vere, and you will feel as you did when we first met that magical night in Paris."

She looked up at him as she spoke, and Kezia thought

it would be impossible for him not to be captivated by *Madame* de Salres' pleading eyes and parted red lips.

She was aware that Perry, who had come in behind her, was looking at her with an expression she had never seen on his face before.

Suddenly she thought how insignificant and tongue-tied she was compared to a woman who could hold both men captive with her inexpressible fascination.

Because she felt unwanted, Kezia walked towards the door.

As she reached it she heard *Madame* de Salres say, again in French:

"Please come out with me, my most adorable, irresistible Vere!"

The way she spoke made Kezia feel as if a thousand knives were being plunged into her breast.

When she reached the hall she started to run, and went on running until she reached her bedroom.

She flung herself down on the bed, and as she did so asked what was wrong and why she should feel as she did.

Then she was afraid of knowing the answer.

* * *

"So that is that!" Perry said as the *Marquis* drove down the drive.

His two outriders followed behind, and *Madame* de Salres' feathers were fluttering in her *chic* and extremely becoming bonnet.

"They . . . said they . . . enjoyed themselves," Kezia said in a small voice.

"I certainly enjoyed having them," Perry replied, "and now I am driving straight to the Bank to deposit this cheque and draw out enough money for the wages and improvements which I intend to put in hand immediately.''

"That sounds wonderful!" Kezia said.

She wondered as she spoke why she did not feel more elated.

Now the *Marquis* and his followers were out of sight, the drive, curving away under the oak trees, seemed somehow empty.

"How could we have imagined for one moment that everything would go off so well?" Perry asked.

"Yes . . . we were very . . . lucky," Kezia agreed.

Perry turned and walked back into the house.

"You will have to hurry and get some new gowns," he said. "There is only a little over two weeks before we leave for France."

"Suppose I fall . . . ill at the . . . last moment?" Kezia suggested in a low voice. "It would then be too . . . late for the *Marquis* to . . . cancel the cheque."

"Oh, for God's sake," Perry said sharply, "you do not want to play tricks with him. He might ask for a refund on what we have already spent! Besides, you will enjoy going to France. Why are you making such a fuss about it?"

"I . . . I am not," Kezia replied, "it is . . . just that . . ."

She stopped.

How could she possibly explain to Perry that she had been quite certain in her mind, although she had no proof of it, that last night the *Marquis* had gone to *Madame* de Salres' bedroom and made love to her.

Just as she had been able to read his thoughts, she was sure that was what had happened.

It was why *Madame* de Salres had come down to dinner in such a good temper.

It was also why she had begged him to go out with her in the moonlight.

Perhaps he had promised to marry her, and Kezia thought that would be the real triumph if she could bring it off.

Perry left her to go to the stables to help get his horses ready so that he could drive his Phaeton to the Bank.

Kezia asked herself why she felt so depressed.

It was easier to say it was the reaction from having so much to do than to face the truth.

Then she remembered how Perry had tried to prevent her from coming in contact with the *Marquis*.

His friend Harry had told him how irresistible to women he was and how they invariably behaved like lunatics because they had fallen in love with him.

"That is how I am behaving," Kezia accused herself, "and how can I torture . . . myself by going . . . to France?"

She knew there was no answer.

As Perry had said, the *Marquis* was so unpredictable that he could easily demand some of his money back.

Alternatively, by some clever means he might manage to cancel the whole transaction.

"I must not offend him . . . I must not," she told herself.

Then a few minutes later she was being even more positive.

"I do . . . not love him! I do not! How could I love anyone who is . . . ruthless and a Norman?"

The answer was quite simple, but she refused to acknowledge it.

Her whole body vibrated to his.

Having said goodbye, he had raised her hand to his lips and had actually kissed it.

Just for a second she had felt the warmth of his mouth

on her skin, and it was as if a shaft of light ran through her whole body.

Because her hand trembled in his, she knew he was aware of it.

Then, despite her resolution not to do so, she had looked into his eyes, and there was nothing else in the world but him.

Finally she went to her mother's room.

The curtains had not been pulled back since she had been there yesterday with the *Marquis*.

"What can I . . . do about him . . . Mama?" she asked, and knew there was no answer to her question.

She went into the wardrobe room next door and wondered which of her mother's gowns she could take with her to France.

It was a waste of their precious money, to spend it on clothes when there were so many other things that had to be bought first.

Then she knew that one part of her mind was telling her to look as lovely as she could for him.

Then, as she thought of *Madame* de Salres in her exquisite gowns, she wanted to laugh at herself for her pretentiousness.

How could the *Marquis* possibly admire anyone so countrified, so unsophisticated, and so foolishly innocent as she was?

She remembered how she had never understood the innuendoes which punctuated *Madame* de Salres' conversation.

Everything she had said seemed to make Perry and the *Marquis* laugh, while she had listened in bewilderment.

She must have seemed like a child, dining for the first

time with the "grown-ups" but unable to take part in or understand what they were saying.

She looked helplessly in her mother's wardrobes, then shut the doors.

'We will be there for only two nights,' she thought. 'I will buy perhaps one evening-gown which is more or less fashionable and something in which to go to the Races.'

She sighed and went on:

'But I will not be extravagant, and I will get one of the women in the village to help me with the alterations to Mama's dresses.'

She could do them quite ably herself, but she thought there were so many other things for her to do.

She was sure that as soon as Perry had given his orders, there would be workmen in the house.

They would have to be supervised and prevented from upsetting Humber and Betsy with the noise and mess they made.

'If I had any sense,' she thought, 'I would have gone into town with Perry, then I could have done some shopping while he was at the Bank.'

Then she told herself that the little Market Town near where they lived would only have gowns that would look frumpish in France.

"It would be much . . . better if I could . . . stay here!" she said aloud.

Even as she spoke and the words seemed to echo in the silence all around her, she knew she wanted to see the *Marquis* again.

She wanted to be with him, she wanted to hear him.

She wanted to see that expression in his eyes which gave her a strange sensation in her breasts.

At last she spoke the words aloud that seemed to be beating within her heart.

"I love . . . him! I love . . . him . . . but please . . . God, help me to try to . . . forget him!''

chapter five

As they neared the *Château* Bayeux, Kezia was convinced that she was dreaming.

When they had boarded the *Marquis'* yacht at Southampton she had been certain then that she was in a Fairy Tale.

So much had happened that she had begun to think that the past was no longer real, and she was already living in the future.

When the *Marquis* and *Madame* de Salres had left, Perry had immediately started to put in hand the repairs to the house.

He had summoned, Kezia thought, every workman in the whole district, and there was pandemonium taking place around them from dawn until dusk.

There were men on the roof, men repairing the windows, and painters and carpenters inside and outside the house.

Perry at the same time began to repair the farm buildings

and told Kezia she was to make a list of what was required in the pensioners' cottages in the village.

This, she thought, was one of the most difficult tasks of all.

The old men and women were so excited about what was happening that they wanted to talk.

What was more, she had to find them accommodation while their cottages were, in some cases, being practically rebuilt.

A week went by before she realised she had had no chance to buy any new clothes in London.

Anyway, it was quite obvious that, if she wanted to do so, Perry would not take her.

She was just thinking despairingly that she would have to find time to alter what was hanging in her mother's wardrobe when she came back to the house for luncheon.

She had been in the village all the morning, and had still only got halfway through her list of what had to be done.

She was late and she hurried the old horse she was riding as quickly as he would go up the drive.

She dismounted at the front door and, taking off his bridle and saddle, left him to find his own way to the stable.

It was something he had done before, and she knew as she had filled his stall early in the morning that he would be eager to get to it.

Perry was already interviewing grooms and talking of buying horses at Tattersalls, but the repairs had to be done first.

Kezia walked in through the front-door to see to her astonishment a huge pile of boxes on the floor.

When she looked at them closely she saw they were dress-boxes.

There were also several round ones, which undoubtedly had been made to contain bonnets.

She stared, and as she did so Dennis, a young man they had engaged from the village to help Old Humber, came into the hall.

"What are these?" Kezia asked him. "And when did they arrive?"

He was a rather slow-witted youth who found it difficult to answer two questions at once.

After a pause, while he was obviously thinking, he said:

"They comes 'bout 'alf-hour ago, Miss, in one o' they Po'-Chaises."

"A Post Chaise!" Kezia exclaimed, knowing that sort of delivery would be very expensive.

Then as she bent down to look at what was written on the label of one of the boxes she read:

"Madame Marie Bertin, 26 Bond Street."

Then Dennis said after a moment:

"There be a letter, Miss, an' Oi puts it on table."

Kezia walked to the table and picked up the envelope, noting when she opened it that the letter inside contained at the top the words:

"Madame Marie Bertin."

Then she read:

"With the compliments of Madame de Salres to thank you for a delightful visit."

She studied the writing, and knew from the way *Madame* de Salres had signed the Visitors' Book that it was not her hand.

Picking up one of the boxes in her arms, she told Dennis to bring up the rest of them to her bedroom.

"Yer luncheon be ready, Miss," he said.

"Bring these up first," Kezia replied.

She knew as she spoke that it would be impossible for her to eat without first having her curiosity assuaged.

She put one of the cardboard boxes down on her bed and opened it, then drew in her breath.

Lying inside was the most beautiful evening-gown she could possibly imagine.

When she lifted it out she found it had a bertha which was of lace delicately embroidered with tiny *diamanté* like dew-drops, and very small pearls.

The skirt that billowed from a tight-fitting waist was as large, if not larger, than those of the gowns worn by *Madame* de Salres.

Only when every dress-box was unpacked did she find she had been given three evening-gowns, three day-dresses, and what she had wanted herself—a travelling gown.

To wear over it when she crossed the Channel was a matching cloak.

Every gown to Kezia screamed the word "Paris."

There was no need for her to be told that *Madame* Bertin must be a very smart and very, very expensive dressmaker to have a shop in Bond Street.

Even before she opened the round boxes to find inside bonnets to match the gowns, she was suspicious.

Yet she knew there was nothing she could do about it.

She was absolutely certain that *Madame* de Salres, who had been polite to her only on the last day of her visit, would not have given her such a magnificent present, even if she could afford to do so.

It would be impossible for her to return the gifts or to accuse the *Marquis*, as she would like to do, of being responsible for them.

If she did so, she was quite certain he would deny it, and only make her look foolish.

Despite the fact that she told herself she should feel angry, if not insulted, by his behaviour, her heart leapt because he had thought of her.

He had been perceptive enough to understand that she would be embarrassed to stay with him in France dressed as she had been when he had last seen her.

She wondered if Perry would believe that *Madame* de Salres was her benefactor.

Then she thought that unless his attention was deliberately drawn to them, he would not even notice the difference in her clothes.

He was obsessed at the moment with the repairs and renovations to the house.

He was so thrilled at being able to afford them that he had even forgotten the necklace and that they had to take it with them to France.

Then the day before they were due to leave it arrived, again by Post Chaise.

With it came a letter from the *Marquis*' Secretary explaining what was arranged for their journey, and Perry was surprised.

"Good Heavens!" he exclaimed. "I had forgotten we were to take the necklace to Bayeux!"

He opened the box to look at it, and said:

"I wonder what would happen if we just kept it as well as the money?"

Kezia gave a cry of horror.

"How can you think of anything so crooked?" she asked.

"I was only joking," Perry replied, "but it must be nice to be as rich as Midas. As far as I can see, he has spent another fortune on the setting."

It was certainly a great improvement as the huge diamonds of the original necklace were now surrounded with smaller ones, and the links between them were also diamonds.

"Would you like to put it on?" Perry suggested.

Kezia shook her head.

"No, I think it is unlucky, and the best place for it is in the Museum, where it will not make any woman so envious as the *Comtesse* was that she tried to steal it."

"If she got as much money as we did for it," Perry replied, "I rather think it was worth it!"

"You are not to think such things!" Kezia said, "and actually, it has been very lucky for us!"

"Very lucky indeed!" Perry agreed seriously. "And because of it the *Marquis* is doing us proud on our journey to Bayeux."

That was an understatement, Kezia thought later, when a Chaise drawn by six horses arrived to convey them to Southampton.

They spent a night on the way staying with the *Marquis'* friend, the Duke of Alderstone.

He was genuinely pleased to see them and arranged a large dinner-party for them to meet his friends.

When they set off the next morning, Kezia knew that part of the enjoyment of the previous evening was that she was so much better dressed than the other ladies present.

For the first time in her life women were looking at her in envy rather than compassion.

The *Marquis'* yacht was large and very comfortable, and it took only three hours to cross the Channel.

When she set foot on French soil, Kezia wondered if they were landing at the same place as the Vikings whose invasion had resulted in the *Marquis* being born with blue eyes.

Perhaps that was also the reason why he was so perceptive.

He was so unlike any man she had ever met before, and she was sure it was because he was a Norman.

He came from a race of men who were trained to use their instinct in battle and on the sea, men who were continually opposing greater forces than themselves.

It sharpened their wits and perhaps at the same time developed their inner vision.

They were able to escape death more easily than other men who did not, or could not use what the Ancient Egyptians called the "Third Eye."

When she thought that was what the *Marquis* had, she gave a little shiver in case he suspected that she had been lying to him.

"Do not forget I am your wife," she had admonished Perry as they set off from the Port in a large and comfortable carriage drawn by four horses.

"I am glad you reminded me," he said, "and for Heaven's sake, be careful of the *Marquis*! Do not forget what Harry told me about him."

"I . . . I have not . . . forgotten," Kezia said in a low voice.

It was something she thought about very often.

In her own way she was being as much of a "lunatic" as the other foolish women who had lost their hearts to a "modern Casanova."

They drove on for a little way, both Kezia and Perry looking out at the countryside.

It was surprisingly like the one they had just left on the other side of the Channel.

Then, for the first time he noticed Kezia's bonnet, and Perry said:

"You look very smart! Where did you get those clothes? I thought you wanted me to take you into London."

"They came from London!" Kezia replied truthfully.

"So you sent for them!" Perry said casually. "That was sensible. I could not have found time to drive you there when there was so much to do at home."

As if the subject no longer interested him, he went on:

"I have just been thinking—if we enlarge the kitchen slightly, it will be much easier for the servants when we give a big party."

Kezia looked at him with frightened eyes.

"A . . . a big party? Oh, Perry, when we have done everything that needs to be done, will we be able to afford it?"

"I am being careful, I really am," he replied, "but I was thinking that when the house looks as it should, I would like to invite some of my friends to stay, and if the *Marquis* can give a Steeple-Chase, so can I!"

"That would be very exciting!" Kezia smiled.

At the same time, she was thinking that if they were not careful, in a year or two they would be in the same position as they had been before the *Marquis* bought the necklace.

For the next few miles she worried a little over the future.

Then when she had her first sight of the *Marquis' Château* she forgot everything but what was happening to her at the moment.

Never had she imagined that anything could be so beautiful and yet so large and imposing.

When they drew a little nearer to it she could see there were five fountains playing in front of the enormous, perfectly-proportioned building.

There was a large fountain in the middle and four others in the formal garden which she had read about in books but never seen before.

Then there were sweeping curved steps leading up to an impressive front-door, and as the carriage drew up beside them, the *Marquis* came out to greet them.

Kezia told herself she must be very controlled and dignified and not let him have the slightest idea what her real feelings were.

But as he raised her hand to his lips and looked at her with his blue eyes, she remembered how handsome he was.

He also had an irresistible force that drew her to him like a magnet.

"You have come!" he said in a low voice. "And you are even more beautiful than I remember!"

She wanted to appear indifferent.

Instead, the colour rose in her cheeks and her eyelashes fluttered because she felt shy.

Although she was not aware of it, she looked unbelievably lovely.

The *Marquis* led them inside the house, and she saw the painted ceilings, the statues and tapestries, and the magnificent array of inlaid French furniture.

It was something about which Kezia had read, and had always wanted to see for herself.

It was all very beautiful, at the same time, she was more concerned with the *Marquis* himself.

She could only listen to his deep voice which had a note of sincerity which she told herself she had to disbelieve.

But it was impossible to think of anything else.

She was not surprised to find at the *Château* a large number of the *Marquis'* relations.

Her mother had told her the French all gathered round the head of the family, who in this case was the *Marquis*.

Kezia was introduced to his mother, who was still beautiful, his grandmother, and a number of cousins.

There was a very attractive dark-haired girl waiting to be introduced.

"This is Lissette—the *Comtesse* de Marnay," the *Marquis* said. "She is my niece and, after she was widowed, came here to live."

"It is much more exciting here with you, Cousin Vere, than at home," she smiled, "where everybody seems to be over eighty!"

The *Marquis* laughed.

"What you really mean," he said, "is that we are nearer to Paris than your parents, and therefore there are more young men to flatter you!"

"What else are men for?" Lissette replied.

Perry laughed as the *Marquis* introduced him.

Kezia was taken upstairs.

When she was shown into her bedroom she had the idea that the *Marquis* had deliberately chosen the most magnificent of his State-Rooms to show her that while the rooms at home were impressive, he could do better.

The ceiling was a riot of cupids chasing Venus, and the bed, with its silk curtains and carved canopy, was like a Papal throne.

The Aubusson carpet was brilliant with roses.

Her luggage had been brought from the yacht in a Brake.

Kezia thought the only things missing were a valet for Perry and a lady's-maid for her.

She was quite certain, however, that the two maids who

were unpacking for her would manage her clothes very much better than any village girl.

She would have been the only maid she could have provided for herself at such short notice.

Because it had taken them almost a day to reach the yacht, cross the Channel, and arrive at the *Château*, Kezia found she was expected to rest before dinner.

Because she had so much to think about, she was glad to do so.

She did not sleep but instructed herself sternly to be very careful not to let the *Marquis* have the slightest suspicion that she was interested in him as a man.

At the same time, she wanted to enjoy every moment of her visit to France because this would never happen again.

She went down to dinner in one of her new gowns.

The expression in the *Marquis'* eyes as she entered the room convinced her without any doubt that it was he who had paid for what she was wearing.

"He had no . . . right to do . . . such a thing!" she told herself.

But when she saw the gowns worn by his relatives she knew how miserable she would have felt if she had come as she had intended.

The gowns which had belonged to her mother were pretty, but completely out of date.

She wore tonight the one she had unpacked first with its beautifully embroidered bertha.

It was white, but at the same time not the white which could be very unbecoming even to a débutante.

The material of the gown had the translucence of a pearl that shimmered in the light of the chandeliers.

The *Marquis* was looking magnificent in his evening-clothes, just as he had when he had stayed with them in England.

His relatives were not over-bejewelled as *Madame* de Salres had been.

But Kezia knew that the diamonds, the pearls, and the other precious stones they wore in their hair and round their necks were priceless.

What was more, they had a family connection in that they had been handed down from generation to generation.

There were twenty people sitting down in the large Banqueting Hall for dinner, and the *Marquis* said to Kezia as they started the meal:

"As I thought you might be tired, it is just a family occasion."

Kezia laughed.

"You must feel lucky to have such a large family?"

"I am lucky," the *Marquis* replied, "because I make sure they obey me and do not dare to argue, whatever I wish to do."

"Then of course you are very spoilt," Kezia teased, "although undoubtedly any Englishman would think you were very fortunate!"

"Are you suggesting that your husband and other men who are married are 'hen-pecked' by their wives?" the *Marquis* enquired.

"I was only thinking of the older generation," Kezia replied. "After all, I suspect that to your mother and your grandmother you will always be a little boy who is getting into mischief."

"That is something I would like to do if you would help me," the *Marquis* said.

She had the idea as he spoke that it was a remark he

might have made to somebody like *Madame* de Salres, with its obvious innuendo.

Instinctively she stiffened.

Because he knew he had made a mistake, he started to tell her the history of some of the pictures that covered the walls.

Then he told her of the legends which had grown up around the *Château* itself.

Because it was so enthralling, they were three-quarters of the way through the meal before Kezia realised that she had not talked to the Gentleman on her other side. Apologetically, she said to him now:

"Please forgive me if I appear to be neglecting you, but I find the history of this beautiful *Château* so enthralling."

"And doubtless, the very eloquent Teller of such tales!" the man replied.

The way he spoke rather surprised Kezia, and when she looked at him she thought there was something she did not particularly like about him.

"Will you tell me who you are?" she asked. "I find it difficult to remember names the first time I hear them."

"I am Orvil de Bayeux," he replied, "and the 'Black Sheep' of the family!"

Kezia laughed.

"Why should you be that?"

"Because I am invariably in trouble," he answered, "and therefore I seldom come home unless I cannot help it!"

Kezia was surprised at his frankness as he went on:

"At the same time, I cannot resist a Steeple-Chase, and as Vere's horses are much better than anything I can afford, I am prepared to ride the best of them. Also I shall enjoy winning one of the prizes he hands out so generously."

Because he seemed to sneer the last words, Kezia asked curiously:

"What sort of prizes?"

"If you are thinking of silver pots and all that nonsense, forget it!" the Frenchman said. "What I intend to win are the gold Louis that are dished out by Vere to every winner—because he can easily afford them!"

Now there was a note of envy and greed in the speaker's voice, and Kezia felt embarrassed.

As if he realised it, Orvil laughed rather unpleasantly.

"I expect, as Guest of Honour, you will help him dispense his family fortune in such an absurd way! While my pockets are empty and I sometimes wonder where my next meal is coming from!"

"I cannot believe that!" Kezia said.

It hurt her to hear the *Marquis* being disparaged in such a way, but Orvil went on:

"It is true, and my only hope is that Vere will continue to remain a bachelor. If he breaks his neck, there is some chance of my inheriting the title and the estate!"

"How can you say such unkind things?" Kezia asked indignantly.

"Are you standing up for him?" Orvil enquired. "In which case, you are obviously besotted by him, like all those other women who hover round him like vultures round a carcass!"

Kezia drew in her breath, and Orvil said mockingly:

"If he fancies you, well, keep him that way! You are married and from my point of view quite harmless!"

He laughed, and it was an unpleasant sound.

"It raised my aunt and my grandmother's hopes for a moment when he came back from England and said he was inviting a new Beauty to stay. They thought it was some nice, innocent girl he might take as his wife, and for a while I was afraid . . ."

"How can you talk like that!" Kezia interrupted.

"But I need not have worried," Orvil went on. "You are married and just like all the others he will tire of you in time, then be looking for another mesmerised little rabbit!"

He sounded so rude that Kezia could hardly believe what she was hearing, even though it sounded better in French than it would have done in English.

As Orvil finished off his glass, which was continually being refilled, she realised he had had too much to drink.

She knew as she turned back to the *Marquis* that he had heard what his brother had said, and she saw the anger in his eyes.

But he only said quietly:

"After dinner I would like to show you some of my pictures."

"I would like to see them, and tomorrow, if there is time, I want to see all over the *Château*."

"There will always be time for us to do the things we really want to do," he replied.

The ladies and gentlemen all left the Dining-Room together.

When they went back to the Salon, Kezia saw that Perry was continuing to talk animatedly as he had been at dinner with Lissette.

As the *Marquis* joined her she said, because it was uppermost in her mind:

"How pretty your niece is! It must have been very sad for her to be widowed so young."

"It would have been," the *Marquis* agreed, "if she had not after two years been disillusioned by her husband."

"Disillusioned?" Kezia queried.

"He was very rich and very spoilt," the *Marquis* said, "and he was also half-Greek."

Kezia looked surprised and he explained:

"His mother was Greek, and because he was her only child she spoilt him abominably with the result that he never considered anybody else but himself.

"So Lissette was unhappy!" Kezia said softly.

"Shall I say she was not unhappy when she was freed from what had been an arranged marriage."

"Now I understand!" Kezia said. "I had forgotten that in France you have arranged marriages, and it is something I think is wrong and can definitely lead to unhappiness."

"That is true," the *Marquis* said quietly.

They walked, as they were talking, towards the end of the room, where hanging on the wall there was a very fine Poussin.

The way he spoke made Kezia think for the first time that perhaps he had been married.

After all, she remembered now that every Empire Aristocrat had his marriage arranged by his family when he was very young.

She wanted to ask him if that was true in his case, but felt shyly it would be an embarrassing question.

As it happened there was no need for her to ask it, for he said:

"As you are thinking, my father arranged my marriage when I was twenty-two."

"And you were unhappy?"

"The wedding did not take place, I am very thankful to say," the *Marquis* replied. "My *fiancée* ran away two weeks before it."

Kezia gave an exclamation.

"Surely that must have been very upsetting for you? It must have made you very unhappy."

"Humiliated, but not unhappy," the *Marquis* replied. "I had suspected from the first moment we became officially engaged that she was not really interested in me but in somebody else."

He paused before he added:

"But in those days I was foolish enough to let other people manipulate me, which is something I have never allowed to happen since!"

There was a note of ruthlessness in his voice which Kezia recognized as he went on:

"It was a merciful deliverance, and I never gambled with my happiness again, thinking it too great a risk."

Kezia thought of Orvil and how unpleasant he had been, and she said impetuously:

"But of course you must marry! You must have a son to inherit this wonderful *Château*, and while there are many women who love you, there must be somebody whom you can love!"

They had stopped in front of a picture, and as she looked at it the *Marquis* said slowly:

"And suppose I was in love with someone I could not marry?"

Kezia thought of *Madame* de Salres and thought that doubtless she had a husband somewhere.

For a moment she tried to think of some way by which he could marry the woman he loved and be happy.

Then, as she thought of him being married, and she was aware that a sharp pain was in her breast, she forced herself to say lightly:

"I thought you were a Norman . . . and therefore a conqueror!"

"Are you really inciting me to take what I want, and damn the consequences?" the *Marquis* asked.

He spoke in English, and because it sounded so very forceful, Kezia laughed.

"Who could resist you riding down from the North pointing your lance?"

"I will answer that question another time," the *Marquis* said unexpectedly. "Now I want you to look at this picture."

With an effort Kezia forced herself to look at the Poussin.

Even as she did so she was aware only of the *Marquis'* vibrations and the strength of him.

"It is a mistake for me to be so near to him," she told herself frantically.

She looked round for Perry, feeling that in some way she should seek his protection.

But he was not with the *Marquis'* relatives who were sitting at the other end of the *Salon*.

There was a window open onto the terrace outside and she knew without being told that Perry and Lissette had gone out into the moonlight.

"Shall we join them?" the *Marquis* asked.

"No, of course not!" Kezia said hastily. "I was only looking for Perry because I know how much he would enjoy seeing this beautiful picture!"

"I am sure he will enjoy it tomorrow," the *Marquis* said.

Kezia realized then that once again he had been reading her thoughts.

Because she was suddenly frightened he would know what she felt about him and how, although she could not even explain it to herself it was like an ecstasy to be near him, she said:

110

"As it has been a long day, and I am tired, will you forgive me if I go upstairs to bed?"

"Yes, of course," the *Marquis* said, "I want you to feel well tomorrow, and I thought if you agree, we could go riding before breakfast, before any of my other guests who are taking part in the Steeple-Chase return."

"I would love that!" Kezia replied.

Suddenly she remembered that among the clothes that *Madame* de Salres had supposedly sent her, there had not been a riding-habit.

She hesitated, thinking of the threadbare skirt and darned blouse she had worn with him at home.

"Will we be riding . . . alone?" she asked, "because I am . . . afraid I will not look very . . . smart."

"I think you will find upstairs everything you require," the *Marquis* said, "and I should have told you before now that you look exactly as I wanted you to."

Kezia looked up at him.

"It was wrong . . . very wrong of you," she said, "but I do not . . . know what I . . . can do . . . about it."

"Why should you do anything but look very, very lovely?" the *Marquis* asked.

Because there was no answer to this, and she was afraid of her own feelings which seemed to flicker through her like little flames of fire, she turned towards the door.

"If I . . . slip away," she said, "perhaps no-one will . . . notice."

"I shall notice," the *Marquis* said. "But tomorrow I shall be waiting in the hall for you at seven o'clock."

He opened the door for her and followed her into the hall.

There were four footmen in attendance, resplendent in elaborate gold-bedecked livery.

Kezia stopped at the foot of the stairs.

"Good night, *Monsieur*," she said softly. "Thank you for a great many things that I must not mention."

"Good night, Kezia," the *Marquis* said.

He raised her hand to his lips and once again she felt his mouth against her skin.

Then, as not only her fingers but her whole body quivered with an inexpressible rapture, she ran up the stairs.

When she reached the landing she wanted to look back, but thought the *Marquis* was watching for her to do so, and it would be a mistake.

Therefore, with her face averted, she walked to her bedroom.

Only when she was out of sight did the *Marquis* slowly and with a strange expression in his blue eyes walk back into the Salon.

chapter six

RIDING over the flat fields beyond the gardens and wood that surrounded the *Château*, Kezia thought she had never been so happy.

As she had anticipated when she looked into her wardrobe after having left the *Marquis* the previous night, she found a riding habit.

It was something else she knew she should refuse if she was behaving properly.

Yet it was impossible not to accept a habit which was different from anything she had seen anywhere.

It was, in fact, so French and so *chic* that it made her thrill just to look at it.

Of a deep blue, it was frogged with white braid.

The lace of the white muslin blouse that went under it was so delicate that she thought it must have been made by the Nuns of a French Convent.

She looked at it for a long time before finally she undressed and got into bed.

Then, as she went over the conversation she had had with the *Marquis*, the rapture she had felt when she had left him downstairs gradually faded.

Of course he was in love with *Madame* de Salres.

If he could not marry her, then he would remain, as he had done so far, an unusual and perhaps unique French bachelor.

But as she loved him she tried to understand how, feeling resentful and in a way frightened by the unhappiness he might have experienced in his arranged marriage, he had decided he would never marry.

What was unthinkable was to know that his place therefore would eventually be taken by his brother Orvil.

Kezia knew he was not only unpleasant, but evil.

It was not only what he said, or the expression of envy and hatred in his eyes.

It was because she could feel emanating from him something which she could describe only as coming from Satan himself.

Ever since she had come to the *Château* she had been vividly aware that her perception reacted very strongly to everything in it, and that included the people.

She was even more aware now of the vibrations from the *Marquis* than she had been when they were in England.

She felt them, too, from his relatives, especially Orvil and Lissette.

She thought that the young widow was the nicest person in the party, with of course the exception of the *Marquis*.

She was glad that Perry could be amused by her rather

114

than by *Madame* de Salres, whom she was certain was a bad woman.

"Why must I be so positive about these people?" she asked.

She could not deny her own inner feelings which had guided her all her life, but never so strongly as they were doing at the moment.

The *Château* was enchanted, she was sure of it, but not just the great rooms.

There was the loveliness of the garden with the water from the fountains making rainbows against the sky.

It was something she felt had perhaps originated with Duke Rollo, and descended down the centuries until it reached the *Marquis*.

"He is a good man . . . despite his . . . reputation," she decided.

She felt herself blush because he had been so generous to her and so understanding as she was sure no other man would have been.

What Englishman would have contrived to provide her with clothes to wear so that she would not feel shabby and inferior with his relatives and friends?

What Englishman would have made their journey so comfortable or remember that she would want to ride, and if she was riding acquire a habit for her?

"How can I not . . . love him?" she asked defiantly.

She felt that Venus and the cupids on the ceiling laughed down at her.

When she finally fell asleep she dreamt of the *Marquis*.

Although when she awoke she could not remember what had happened in her dream, she felt he was near her.

His face was so engraved on her mind that she could almost see him.

* * *

At exactly seven o'clock Kezia ran down the stairs to find the *Marquis* waiting for her in the hall.

She knew that, in her new habit which fitted her exactly and accentuated her figure, she looked very different from the way she had in England.

She saw his eyes flicker over her, and she said a little shyly:

"I know it is . . . incorrect and . . . perhaps wrong . . . but there is nothing I can . . . do about it."

"Nothing!" he agreed. "And now the horses are waiting."

There appeared to be nobody else in the party to join them, and there were only two horses waiting outside.

The *Marquis* lifted her into the saddle.

Despite her every resolution, Kezia felt herself thrill as his hands touched her and she was close to him.

Then, as she lifted the reins, she tried to think of nothing but the horse she was riding.

They did not speak until they had galloped for quite a long distance.

Then the *Marquis* pulled in his stallion and Kezia did the same with hers.

"That was wonderful!" she exclaimed.

Then, as her eyes met the *Marquis*', she looked away quickly and told herself not to be beguiled by anything he said or by the way he was looking at her.

"He loves *Madame* de Salres!" she murmured beneath

her breath. "And he compliments every woman he is with, so I would be very foolish to believe him!"

They walked their horses a little way, then the *Marquis* said:

"I want you to turn round and look at the *Château* from here. It is, in my opinion, the best view of my home."

Obediently Kezia turned her horse.

The *Marquis* was right!

The *Château* looked so magnificent and at the same time so beautiful that she thought it must be a mirage.

She could see the sun glinting on its windows and the water from the fountain, and beyond there were the trees.

As she looked, a flight of white doves, which she had noticed in the garden, flew across the *Château*.

There were quite a number of them, and the *Marquis* said softly:

"The birds which belong to Aphrodite."

"They are beautiful, like everything else with which you have surrounded yourself," Kezia remarked, "so how could you not be happy?"

The *Marquis* was looking at the *Château*, and after a moment he said:

"I am often lonely in my heart!"

He did not have to explain. Kezia knew instinctively exactly what he meant.

He might be surrounded by people, but there was something missing: something spiritual which they could not give him, not even the beautiful ladies with whom he spent so much of his time.

Then she asked herself why was that true?

Before she could formulate the question to ask him for an explanation, he said:

"I think you are aware that while in our passage through

life we encounter love in one form or another, it is rarely the perfection we seek.''

He spoke so seriously that Kezia was surprised, and she answered:

''I know . . . very little about love . . . but I think I understand that perhaps because you are more . . . demanding and more . . . fastidious than other men . . . what you are . . . offered is . . . not enough.''

She thought as she spoke of the women who had laid their hearts at his feet.

They had become, as Harry had said, so obsessed by him that they were lunatics where he was concerned.

She wondered why he could not love at least one of them as overwhelmingly as they obviously loved him.

''I know what you are thinking,'' the *Marquis* said, ''but I can swear to you, Kezia, that I have tried to find a woman who not only captures my heart, but also my soul.''

''Perhaps . . . you are . . . asking . . . too much!'' Kezia suggested hesitatingly.

''It happens to other men,'' the *Marquis* objected, ''so why not to me?''

He spoke sharply, almost harshly, and Kezia said:

''You are still young and you must go on reaching for the stars even though if you touch them you may be disappointed.''

''I am quite certain that if I touched the star I am seeking I would not be disappointed,'' the *Marquis* said firmly. ''In fact, it would be the miracle for which I have prayed.''

It seemed so strange that he should pray as she had.

She prayed every night that one day she would find a man whom she loved and who loved her in the same way as her father and mother had loved each other.

They had been so happy and complete in themselves.

"Are you surprised," the *Marquis* asked again in a hard voice that seemed to Kezia somewhat hurtful, "that I should pray?"

"I am just a little . . . surprised that you . . . admit to it," Kezia replied. "Most men would be too shy to say so."

"I am not shy," the *Marquis* said, "and I have prayed that I shall find the love that I seek and it will not be out of reach."

Again it flashed through Kezia's mind that he was thinking of *Madame* de Salres.

Because she loved him and because she wanted him to have what he wanted in life she said softly:

"I too will . . . pray that you will . . . find what you are . . . seeking, the miracle will happen and it can be yours."

"Thank you," the *Marquis* said quietly, "and I have the feeling, Kezia, that your prayer will be heard!"

Then, as if there were nothing more to say, he turned his horse.

As Kezia did the same, they went off at a gallop, jumping several hedges in quick succession.

When they arrived back at the *Château* Kezia's cheeks were flushed and her eyes were shining with happiness.

She only wished she could go on riding with the *Marquis* for ever, perhaps to some distant horizon where the world came to an end and there would be a Heaven which would be theirs for eternity.

She knew she was only romancing, and there was a great deal for him to do today, and she was lucky to have been with him alone.

She ran upstairs to her bedroom to change.

She was just putting on one of her pretty gowns without

bothering to ring for the maid when there was a knock on her door and Perry came in.

He was dressed in riding-clothes and looked, she thought, particularly handsome, at the same time, very English.

"I am just going down to breakfast," he said, "then to the stables to choose which horse I shall ride today. The *Marquis* has told me I can have any one I want, except for the one he requires himself."

"Oh, Perry, how wonderful!" Kezia exclaimed. "But hurry, in case the *Marquis*' brother Orvil takes the best before you get there."

"Orvil!" Perry exclaimed. "I think he is an unpleasant chap, and the *Comtesse* told me last night that he is disliked by the whole family and causes scandal after scandal in Paris."

"It must be very worrying for the *Marquis*," Kezia murmured.

"I suppose he has to have some problems, considering how much he has, and how rich he is!" Perry remarked.

There was a note of envy in her brother's voice which made Kezia say quickly:

"Do not speak like Orvil de Bayeux, who was horrible last night, and anyway, had too much to drink!"

"Have nothing to do with him," Perry said sharply, "and for Heaven's sake, Kezia, do not fall in love with the *Marquis*!"

Kezia did not reply, and he went on:

"Harry warned us what he was like, and although there is no sign of *Madame* de Salres, I expect either she or another woman like her will be waiting for the *Marquis* in Paris, where he will return as soon as this party is over."

Kezia felt a pain in her breast at the thought of it. Then in defence of the *Marquis* she said:

"You seem quite content to like him at the moment!"

As she spoke she was aware that Perry looked at her sharply.

"If he is making love to you," he said, "you are not to listen. Do you understand, Kezia? I am not having you breaking your heart over a Frenchman whose reputation is disgraceful from an English point of view!"

Kezia turned towards the dressing-table.

"We have delivered the necklace," she said, "and I suppose we are going home tomorrow, so I will never see him again."

"And a good thing too!" Perry said. "At the same time, I have asked the *Comtesse* to come to stay with us as soon as the house is finished."

"The *Comtesse*?" Kezia asked.

"Lissette," Perry said. "She says she has never been to England, and I think she would enjoy staying with us."

He went from the room as he spoke and Kezia looked after him in surprise.

Then she told herself it would be very nice for Perry to have somebody like Lissette to stay.

Perhaps it would mean that he would not be so anxious to go to London, where he gambled with his rich friends.

Also, although he would not talk about it, she was sure he entertained a lot of women of whom her mother would not have approved.

Then as she looked at her reflection in the mirror she told herself that Perry was right; she must not listen to the *Marquis*.

If they talked as they had this morning, in a way she had never talked to a man before, she would miss him even more despairingly than she would do at the moment.

"I love . . . him!" she said in a whisper. "But it is only

because I am a . . . foolish girl from the . . . country who has never seen . . . a man like him before!''

She had the uncomfortable feeling that it was something she would not know again, in which case she would remain an Old Maid for the rest of her life.

Because the idea was so frightening, she jumped up and ran downstairs to breakfast.

The old Ladies were obviously having breakfast in their rooms.

There was Lissette and one other young woman amongst the men who were seated round the table in the Breakfast-Room.

The *Marquis* was at the head of it, and as he stood up as Kezia entered, he indicated the chair next to his.

There was therefore nothing she could do but sit where he had suggested.

She was offered several dishes, and when she had taken all she required the *Marquis* said:

''I am sure you are hungry, I know I am! You must therefore eat as much as you can, as luncheon will be late.''

''The food here is so delicious,'' Kezia said, ''that I know if I stayed here for long I should grow very fat!''

She thought as she spoke of how little she and the Humbers had to eat before the *Marquis* had come to stay.

It was only thanks to him that for a little while, at any rate, she would not be worrying where the next meal was to come from.

''It is something that must not happen again,'' the *Marquis* said quietly.

She was aware that once again he knew what she was thinking.

Because it was embarrassing to think he had provided them with so much, even though he had obtained the necklace by doing so, she blushed and looked away from him.

Then, to her consternation, Orvil rose from where he had been sitting to come and sit next to her as he had done last night.

"I hear, Lady Falcon," he said, "that you had *Madame* de Salres staying with you in your house in England."

"Yes, she came with your brother," Kezia replied.

"I am surprised that a woman of that sort should be acceptable in a respectable English house!"

Kezia did not answer, and Orvil went on:

"I saw her yesterday, and she was very surprised that you had come to France with your husband."

"She was aware that the *Marquis* had asked us to bring the necklace he had acquired for his Museum."

Orvil made a sound of disgust.

"His Museum!" he exclaimed. "My brother wastes his money on buying a lot of nonsensical objects instead of spending the money as he should on his relatives!"

'And one relative in particular!' Kezia thought to herself, although she knew it would be a mistake to say so.

"I am sure *Madame* de Salres will be interested to hear," Orvil went on, "that you enjoyed your ride this morning. She is, of course, extremely jealous where my brother is concerned."

Kezia did not know what to say.

She knew he was being deliberately provocative, and his insinuations and the sneering way he spoke made her feel very uncomfortable.

She was certain he would enjoy upsetting *Madame* de Salres by exaggerating the importance of her riding alone with the *Marquis*.

Because he hated his brother, he was out to make trouble.

She wondered if she should plead with him to do nothing

of the sort, but was sure he would not listen to her.

Instead, she went on eating her breakfast, finding the food of which she had been deprived for so long now tasted like sawdust.

It was with a great sense of relief when she realized that Orvil, finding he could not make her reply to his rudeness, had risen to his feet.

"I am going to the stables, Vere," he said, "in the hope of selecting one of your much-vaunted horses to carry me to victory!"

"The choice is yours!" the *Marquis* said. "And, of course, Orvil, I wish you luck!"

"You wish me nothing of the sort!" Orvil sneered. "But I shall be delighted, as you well know, to take any money I can get out of you!"

He walked from the room after he had spoken.

Although the *Marquis* said nothing, one or two of his guests murmured amongst themselves and Kezia knew they were shocked at the way Orvil de Bayeux was behaving.

She was not surprised as soon as he had gone when Perry also rose.

As he did so she heard him say to Lissette:

"You promised to help me choose the best horse in the stable, and I cannot manage without you!"

"I will show you the ones which Uncle Vere thinks are the best," Lissette replied.

They left the room together, and as they shut the door behind them the *Marquis* said to Kezia:

"I hope you do not mind my niece helping your husband."

Kezia smiled.

"It would be wonderful for Perry if he could win one of

your races, but even without winning, it is a great experience for him to ride horses as fine as yours!''

''If I had thought of it I would have organised a Ladies' Race,'' the *Marquis* said, ''which you undoubtedly would have won.''

Kezia laughed.

''I am quite happy, after riding this morning, to be a spectator, and if I did win, perhaps the other entries would be jealous, and that would be a mistake.''

She wondered as she spoke if *Madame* de Salres was a rider.

She thought it unlikely, as she had not wished to ride when she was staying with them in England.

The *Marquis* rose to his feet.

''Come along,'' he said to the other gentlemen seated round the table, ''I think we ought to go down to the race course, as the riders who are not staying here should be arriving by now.''

He looked at Kezia and added:

''There will always be a carriage at the front-door to convey you or anybody else to the course when they wish to watch the proceedings.''

''Thank you,'' Kezia smiled.

The gentlemen left the Breakfast-Room and a Lady who was a cousin of the *Marquis* moved up to sit in the chair beside her.

''I have not seen Vere look so happy or be so enthusiastic about anything for a long time,'' she said.

Kezia looked at her in surprise.

''I should have thought from all I have heard about him,'' she said, ''that he is a very happy man.''

''Not always when he is at home,'' the cousin remarked, whose name Kezia had learnt was Teresa.

"Why is that?" Kezia asked.

"I think it is because he finds it lonely being the head of a large family," Teresa explained. "He continually has them either begging him for money, fighting with each other, or pleading with him to marry and have an heir."

"And that makes him unhappy?"

"You too would be unhappy if you had Orvil as a brother," Teresa said frankly.

"I . . . I can see he is . . . somewhat of a problem," Kezia agreed.

She spoke hesitatingly, choosing her words with care.

She knew it would be a great mistake for her to seem to be too involved with the *Marquis'* affairs or to criticise one of his family, even somebody as unpleasant as his brother.

"To tell the truth," Teresa said, "I am very sorry for Cousin Vere, and I am not surprised he spends so much of his time in Paris."

'With *Madame* de Salres!' Kezia added silently.

She felt again the pain that was somehow agonising in her breast.

*   *   *

The race was exciting, and Kezia enjoyed every moment of it.

She watched with delight as Perry won a race by a neck from ten other entrants.

Lissette, who was sitting beside Kezia, clapped her hands and jumped up and down with excitement.

"I told him that was the best horse in the stables," she said, "and he snatched it right from under the nose of Cousin Orvil, who was determined to win this race!"

It was quite obvious he was furious at not having done so.

As the riders came back from the course, Kezia thought she had never seen a man look so angry.

She only hoped he would not be disagreeable to Perry.

She could see Perry dismounting his horse and talking to Lissette animatedly about his win.

It had been an important race, and when Kezia heard that the prize was the equivalent in *francs* of five hundred pounds, she could hardly believe it.

How had they been so lucky as not only to sell the necklace to the *Marquis* but now for Perry to have won five hundred pounds from him?

She had a feeling it was too much and they should not take it.

At the same time, she knew that both men would laugh at her if she said so.

The Steeple-Chase was to take place after luncheon.

Perry, having won the first race, it was only fair that the winner should be a neighbour, so Orvil was once again disappointed.

When they went back to the *Château* for luncheon, the *Marquis* told the ladies of the house-party to distribute themselves amongst the guests who were not staying in the house.

Kezia found herself sitting next to a man older than most of the riders.

She had learnt that when he was young he was one of the most acclaimed horsemen in France.

"Your husband, *Madame*, did very well this morning," he said.

"I am very honoured to hear you say so," Kezia replied.

The man, whose name was the *Comte* d' Outeur, smiled.

"So you have heard of me?"

127

"Yes, *Monsieur*, and I am very impressed."

"I am too old these days to do too much racing," he said, "but de Bayeux insisted that I should take part in his Steeple-Chase and it is something I will greatly enjoy, although I have no illusions about winning it."

"I have a feeling the *Marquis* will do that himself," Kezia said.

"I shall be disappointed if he does not," the *Comte* replied, "and in this neighbourhood, it will be a very popular win."

Kezia must have looked surprised, for he said:

"I expect you have been told a lot of rubbish about de Bayeux. The trouble with women is that they talk too much. I can assure you he is an excellent Landlord and, in my opinion, a credit to Normandy! In fact, we are exceedingly proud of him."

Kezia felt her heart warm at such glowing words.

Then, as she looked at the *Marquis* at the top of the table, she found that he was looking at her.

She felt at that moment as if they were united with each other over time and space.

Then one of the ladies beside him attracted his attention, and he turned away.

It was then she knew that, despite all the warning she had been given, he held her heart completely.

She would never, however long she lived, love anybody else.

As soon as everybody had received their prizes and the guests from outside had returned home, Kezia went upstairs to lie down on her bed.

She was almost asleep when the door opened and Perry came in.

He crossed the room to sit down on the side of the bed facing her.

"I want to talk to you," he said.

"I am so glad you won that big prize!" she said. "And you rode brilliantly!"

"It is all due to Lissette," he said, "and that is what I want to talk to you about."

"You told me she wanted to visit England," Kezia said.

There was silence. Then Perry said bluntly:

"I think I have fallen in love!"

Kezia's eyes opened wide, and she sat up in bed.

"Fallen in love? Oh, Perry . . . is it possible . . . so quickly?"

Even as she spoke she knew the answer.

Her own father and mother had fallen in love with each other the moment they had first met.

She also knew, if she was honest, that it was what had happened to her when she met the *Marquis*.

"I love her!" Perry said firmly. "And now I am wondering how I can tell her that you and I are not husband and wife, but brother and sister."

Kezia gave a little cry.

"Oh, Perry! Do be careful! The *Marquis* may be furious if he realizes we have deceived him, and I am sure his mother and grandmother would be shocked!"

"Then what the devil am I to do?" Perry asked.

He got off the bed to walk restlessly round the room.

"I had always thought all that talk about 'love at first sight' was a lot of rubbish, but now I know that it is true! I have not yet said anything really serious to Lissette, but I could swear that she feels the same way I do."

"Perhaps," Kezia suggested slowly, "you should wait and tell her when she comes to visit us in England?"

"And have her snapped up by some other man because she thinks I am not available?" Perry asked.

"Then what do you intend to do?" Kezia questioned in a frightened voice.

"I shall tell her the truth, and swear her to secrecy," Perry replied, "but I thought it only fair to tell you first what I was intending to do."

"Oh, Perry, you must make her promise that she will not tell the *Marquis* until after we have left tomorrow."

"All right," Perry agreed, "but I have no wish to leave if the *Marquis* asks me to stay."

"I think we should go home," Kezia said, "you know how much there is for you to do."

She saw her brother was indecisive and said:

"The sooner we can get the house in order, the sooner Lissette can come to stay."

She saw Perry's eyes brighten, then he said:

"You do not suppose she will think we are not as comfortable as they are here?"

"And never will be, however hard we try," Kezia laughed. "You know, Perry, that we cannot compete with the *Marquis* or the *Château*."

Perry smiled a little wryly, then he said:

"You forget Lissette is French, and she told me last night at dinner she is a very good cook!"

"As long as she has the right things with which to cook, you will be in clover!"

She thought as she spoke how hard it had been at times to find anything to eat.

It was only after Perry had gone to his own room that she remembered that Lissette was very rich.

She sent up a little prayer to her mother that, if Perry

was in love, he could marry Lissette and they would be happy together.

She thought it would solve his problems.

Then she thought of herself, and knew that when Perry married it would be a great mistake for her to stay in the house where she had been the mistress.

Beside which, both Perry and Lissette were young and would want to be alone together.

"I shall have to find . . . somewhere to . . . go," she murmured.

She thought of the relation who was going to present her to the Social World.

If she went to London, and could not afford the many gowns that would be required for a *débutante*, that would be no solution.

Then she also knew that leaving the *Marquis* she no more wished to go to Balls or for that matter to be a social success.

"Perhaps I could find a cottage in the village or on the estate," she told herself.

She felt suddenly that her whole world had turned upside-down and she was alone!

* * *

The maids came to tell her it was time to dress for dinner, and she wore the second of the beautiful gowns which had come for her from Bond Street.

It was different from the one she had worn last night.

Of very pale green, almost the colour of her eyes, it was trimmed with a heavy lace bertha, and there was lace decorating the full skirt.

It was plain, and yet extremely smart, and gave her a

grace which made her look as if she had just stepped in from the woods outside the *Château*.

She had already been told that Frenchmen were interested in women's clothes and had excellent taste.

She thought when she looked at herself in the mirror that if the *Marquis* had chosen her gowns, that was true.

As they had been such a large party at luncheon, tonight they were only twelve at dinner; several of the relatives had left when the races were over.

"Have you enjoyed yourself today?" the *Marquis* asked Kezia, who was sitting next to him as she had last night.

"Every moment!" she answered enthusiastically. "And you organised everything . . . brilliantly!"

"That is the sort of compliment I like to receive!" he replied.

He was looking, she thought, even more handsome than usual.

The sun which had been very strong in the afternoon had darkened his skin a little and made him look, she thought, even more like a man who had fought a battle in the heat of the day, or ridden against an enemy on a fiery steed.

Then she told herself she must not concentrate on the *Marquis*.

Yet, knowing she was to leave tomorrow, she wanted to have as many memories of him as possible.

It would be all she would have, she thought, to sustain her in the future.

To her relief, Orvil was sitting at the other end of the table.

She did not have to listen to his sneering remarks, but she was aware that, when he looked at his brother, it was with a very unpleasant expression in his eyes.

Perry and Lissette, who were sitting next to each other,

seemed to have a great deal to say, and for all intents and purposes had forgotten that anybody else existed.

She saw the *Marquis'* mother look at them once or twice in surprise and she wondered how she could warn Perry to be more discreet.

Then she told herself that whatever happened, after tonight it was immaterial, and tomorrow they would be leaving.

Then perhaps the *Marquis* would go to Paris to see *Madame* de Salres.

"It is . . . all over!" Kezia told herself. "And the . . . sooner I try . . . to forget . . . the better!"

"What are you thinking about?" the *Marquis* asked unexpectedly.

Kezia told him the truth.

"I was wondering what time we have to leave tomorrow, and if we shall have the privilege of crossing the Channel again in your yacht."

"It will be waiting for you whenever you are ready to go," he said, "but—must you leave me so quickly?"

Kezia felt her heart leap.

Then before she could answer he went on:

"There are so many things I want to show you now . . . the Steeple-Chase is finished, and you have not chosen the horse I am going to give you, or seen all of the *Château*."

"I want to see it," Kezia replied in a low voice, "but . . . Perry and I thought you had . . . asked us for only two nights."

"Then you were mistaken," the *Marquis* said, "and I will speak to your husband after dinner."

As everybody left the Dining-Room, Kezia saw Perry and Lissette slip away while everyone went into the Salon.

She thought it was a mistake, but there was nothing she could do.

The *Marquis*' mother was pouring out the coffee, and she hoped their absence would not cause comment.

She refused coffee, feeling it would keep her awake and she had no wish to lie for hours in the darkness thinking of him.

He came to her side to hand her a small glass of liqueur, saying:

"I want you to try this because it is made by the monks, and I think you will enjoy it."

Kezia took a small sip and found it was sweet and delicious.

"There is another place I thought you might like to visit," he went on. "It is only a small Monastery, but it has been on my land for three-hundred years, and the Chapel is very beautiful."

"I would . . . love to . . . see it!" Kezia replied.

"And so you shall, but first you must inspect the *Château* and there is one picture I particularly want to show you. Shall we go to look at it now?"

Kezia put down on a small table the glass of liqueur from which she had taken only a few sips.

The *Marquis* put his empty coffee-cup back on the silver tray beside which his mother was sitting.

As he did so his brother Orvil did the same thing, and for a moment the two brothers were standing side by side.

As Kezia looked at them, she could not help thinking what a difference there was between them.

'It might almost be a picture,' she thought, 'of Cain and Abel, or of Good and Evil.'

Then as Orvil made some remark to the *Marquis* which

she was sure was rude, the door suddenly opened and a servant announced:

"*Madame* de Salres, *Monsieur*!"

The *Marquis* stiffened in astonishment while everybody else's head turned towards the door.

Slowly, dressed flamboyantly in a red gown and glittering with a profusion of diamonds, *Madame* de Salres stood for a moment in the doorway looking at the assembled guests.

Then slowly she walked down the room towards them, her eyes on the *Marquis*.

She was carrying in her hand a bouquet of white orchids, which seemed strange.

But Kezia thought she intended to present them to the *Marquis*' mother as an apology for arriving uninvited.

Then, as she almost reached the *Marquis*, she stopped, and, addressing him in French, she said:

"*Bonsoir, Mon Cher*! I see that your brother Orvil is right and that you have the Englishwoman for whom you neglected me when we were together in that most uncomfortable of houses."

The way she spoke was, Kezia thought, deliberately insulting, and the *Marquis* took a step forward to say:

"Now, listen, Yvonne . . ."

"I am not listening to you!" *Madame* de Salres interrupted. "I have come here to inform you, if you do not know it already, that you have broken my heart, and despite the lies you told me to keep me from making a scene when we were in England, I know that you have thrown me aside, as you have thrown so many other women before me!"

"I will not listen to this!" the *Marquis* began.

"You will listen," *Madame* de Salres said, her voice rising, "because there is nothing else you can do about it! You will listen to me and I will show you, my most noble

Marquis, that you cannot play every woman false and get away with it. In fact, I intend to ensure there will be no more women in your life, now or ever!''

She almost shrieked the last words, and as the *Marquis* took a step towards her, *Madame* de Salres pulled her right hand from under the bouquet.

In it she held a pistol.

She was pointing it at the *Marquis*, who stood still, looking at her.

''Do not be foolish, Yvonne!'' he said very quietly. ''If you kill me, you will stand trial for murder!''

''I know that,'' *Madame* de Salres replied, but she smiled and somehow it contorted her lips. ''I will not kill you, *Mon Brave,* no! But you will suffer, and there will be no more women in your life!''

It was then Kezia knew what she was about to do.

Even as *Madame* de Salres took aim with the pistol, pointing it at the *Marquis* below his waist, she threw herself against her.

She forced her arm away from the *Marquis*, but it was, however, too late!

As she did so, *Madame* pulled the trigger and the explosion seemed to echo deafeningly through the Salon.

There was a scream from one of the ladies.

Then slowly, very slowly, Orvil de Bayeux fell backwards onto the carpet.

chapter seven

For a moment everybody seemed turned to stone.

Then the *Marquis* stretched out to take the smoking pistol from *Madame* de Salres' hand.

As he did so, she turned and, screaming at the top of her voice, ran down the Salon towards the door.

Galvanised into action, two of the men in the party bent over Orvil, but Kezia did not see them.

She felt a sudden darkness enveloping her, and she put out her hands to hold on to something which was not there.

She would have fallen had not the *Marquis* thrown the pistol he was holding into a chair and picked her up in his arms.

He did not speak to anybody.

He merely carried her down the room and, as his relatives behind him all started to talk at once, he went out into the hall.

He almost bumped into a *Valet de chambre* who was just about to enter the *Salon*.

"There was a shot, *Monsieur!*" he exclaimed.

"Send a groom immediately for the Doctor!" the *Marquis* ordered.

He walked on and started to ascend the stairs.

He was halfway up them before Kezia regained consciousness.

She could not for the moment remember what had happened but felt as if she were deafened by the noise of the shot that was still echoing in her ears.

Then as she realized who held her she said in a small, hesitating voice:

"She . . . she . . . would have . . . killed you!"

"But you saved me," the *Marquis* said quietly.

He walked along the passage, pushed open the door to Kezia's bedroom and, carrying her in, laid her down gently on the bed.

"Y-you are not . . . hurt?"

He did not answer, he only bent over her, looking at her pale face, her frightened eyes, and her trembling lips.

Then his mouth came down on her.

He kissed her very gently, but Kezia felt as if her whole body came alive.

Without meaning to, she tried to move closer to him, and the *Marquis'* lips became more possessive, more insistent.

Then, as Kezia felt as if they were surrounded by a dazzling light which was shining in her body and seeping through her breasts up to her lips, the *Marquis* raised his head.

For a moment his eyes held hers captive.

Incoherently in a voice he could hardly hear she asked:

"Sh-she . . . has not . . . h-hurt you?"

"You saved me," the *Marquis* said again, "and now I must go down to see what is happening."

Kezia's hands moved, but she did not touch him.

"Do . . . not . . . leave me," she whispered.

"I will come back," the *Marquis* promised, "just rest and try to forget what has happened."

He looked down at her as if he would imprint her beauty on his mind. Then he went from the room, closing the door behind him.

Kezia shut her eyes.

Could it really have happened?

Had she been in a nightmare in which *Madame* de Salres had tried to injure the *Marquis* and by the mercy of God she had been able to save him?

Vaguely she remembered that before she had fainted Orvil had moved, or had he fallen?

She wondered if the shot had wounded him.

Then she remembered that *Madame* de Salres had said it was Orvil who had told her that she was staying in the *Château*.

He must have been determined to make trouble for his brother because he hated him.

"Please . . . God . . . do not let . . . him hurt the *Marquis*," she prayed.

Then it was impossible to think of anything but the wonder of his kiss, and the incredible rapture it had given her.

She had never imagined a kiss would be like that!

Or that it could evoke an ecstasy that was indescribable and make her feel that she was flying in the sky and the angels were singing.

"I love . . . him! I love . . . him!" she said as she had a

hundred times last night lying in the same bed as she was now.

Then she remembered that she had thought he loved *Madame* de Salres.

Although he might feel ashamed and humiliated at the way she had behaved, he could still have an affection for her.

But whatever he felt for anybody else, he had kissed her!

Kezia knew that if she never saw him again after she returned to England, he had captured her heart, drawn it from her body, and it was no longer her own.

Because the rapture of the *Marquis'* kiss made it impossible to think of anything else, she lay quietly for a long time.

Then the door opened and he came back.

Even before she opened her eyes she knew he was there.

She could feel a throbbing sensation in her breast and an inexpressible joy which ran through her like sunlight.

Then he was sitting facing her and he asked in his deep voice:

"Are you all right?"

Kezia looked up into his blue eyes and reached out her hand.

"What has . . . happened?" she asked in a whisper.

The *Marquis* held her hand closely in both of his.

"Although the bullet was meant for me," he said, "because you thrust the pistol aside, it hit my brother Orvil!"

Kezia's fingers tightened on his.

"Is . . . is he . . . dead?"

"Not yet," the *Marquis* replied, "but the wound is very near his heart, and it is unlikely he will live long."

Kezia felt as if she had stopped breathing. Then she said:

"It was . . . my fault . . ."

"But you saved me!" the *Marquis* said quietly. "And if Yvonne de Salres had killed me, as she might have done, it would have been a *crime passionnel*, which is permissible in France."

Kezia was looking up at him, and now she was frightened, very frightened.

"What I have told my family who fortunately were the only people present," the *Marquis* said, "is that it was a regrettable accident and they are all to agree that *Madame* de Salres had brought me an ancient pistol from my Museum and had no idea it was loaded."

"That . . . is a . . . clever . . . explanation," Kezia murmured.

"Luckily neither Lissette nor your husband were present, and everybody who was is very aware that it would be a great mistake for any of us to be involved in a scandal."

"And if . . . your brother . . . dies?" Kezia asked.

"He will linger, I think, for several days. But there will be no need for us to inform the Police, and it will just be a 'regrettable accident.' "

"I am . . . so glad," Kezia said, "for . . . your . . . sake."

She thought as she spoke that anything which harmed or upset the *Marquis* was wrong.

He was so handsome, so overwhelmingly magnificent that a scandal would be worse for him than for anybody ordinary and of no consequence.

She tried not to think of Yvonne de Salres and her screaming voice as she had run from the Salon.

The *Marquis* read her thoughts.

"Forget her!" he said. "She was a mistake, and I have been punished for making it. I wanted your visit here with me to be as happy and as beautiful as you are yourself."

Because of the deep note in his voice, as he spoke the

colour came back to Kezia's face and her eyelashes fluttered because she was shy.

The *Marquis'* hand on hers tightened as he said:

"I have something to ask you, Kezia, something which matters to me more than anything else in the world!"

He spoke so seriously that she looked up at him in surprise.

Then he said very quietly:

"I love you! Will you come away with me and I swear to you by everything I hold sacred that the moment your husband divorces you, we will be married!"

For a moment Kezia just stared at him, finding it hard to understand the enormity of what he had just asked her.

He was waiting for her answer.

She thought it would not be true that the *Marquis* de Bayeux, whose title was one of the most important in France, whose family went back to the great Duke Rollo, was actually prepared to marry a woman who had been divorced.

She knew that no man could make a greater sacrifice for love.

Once again she felt as if he carried her up to the sky and the light that had been there when he kissed her enveloped them both.

Then she drew in a deep breath and said in a voice that was like the song of a bird:

"I love you . . . I love you so much . . . that I do not . . . know how to . . . tell you . . . that . . ."

"That is all I need to know," the *Marquis* interrupted.

He bent forward and then he was kissing her.

Now it was not the gentle kiss he had given her before, but his lips were possessive and demanding.

Just for a moment, as if he lost control of himself, he was kissing her as a conqueror.

He was the victor, as a man who had fought a desperate battle, and had at the last moment turned defeat into victory.

Only when they were both breathless and Kezia felt as if it were impossible to feel such ecstasy and not die of the wonder of it, did he raise his head.

"You are mine!" he said fiercely. "Mine, as I meant you to be from the first moment I saw you, and no one shall take you from me!"

Then he was kissing her again, and only when it was difficult to breathe did she make a little movement.

He took his lips from hers.

"Forgive me, my precious," he said, "but I have been in hell these last few days, thinking you were out of reach and I would never be able to make you love me."

"And I was . . . so afraid you were . . . reading my thoughts . . . and would know . . . how much . . . I . . . loved you," Kezia said.

The *Marquis*' lips found hers again, but after a moment she pushed him a little way from her.

"I . . . I have . . . something to . . . tell you."

"There is no need for words," the *Marquis* said. "All we have to decide, you and I, is how soon we can go away together and leave all the explanations and recriminations to take place after we have gone, when we will not be here to hear them."

Kezia knew he was thinking of Perry.

Because it was so wonderful that there would be no recriminations, she could not think of the words in which to tell the *Marquis* there was no need for them to disappear.

"What I have planned," he was saying, "is that we will take my yacht and seek, my darling, the first horizon you

143

told me you wished to find. Then travel to the horizon beyond it, and the others beyond that.''

Kezia opened her lips to speak, but he went on:

"I have so much to give you, so much to teach you, especially about love.''

He bent nearer to her as he asked:

"How can you be so innocent and unspoilt? If I did not know you were married, I would swear you have never been kissed until I kissed you after you had saved me from the bullet that would have crippled me.''

"You . . . are quite . . . right,'' Kezia whispered, "I never . . . have . . . been!''

The *Marquis* was still.

"What do you mean—I do not understand.''

"I . . . I never . . . have been . . . kissed by anyone . . . but you!''

"That is—impossible!''

In a very small voice Kezia said:

"Perhaps . . . you will be . . . angry when you . . . hear the . . . truth.''

"The truth?'' the *Marquis* questioned.

"P-Perry . . . is my . . . brother!''

As she spoke, Kezia felt a sudden terror in case, because they had been so deceitful, the *Marquis* would be shocked and stop loving her.

For a second she could not look at him.

"Your brother!'' he exclaimed.

Because she was frightened she looked up pleadingly.

"F-forgive me . . . please . . . forgive me, but Perry thought it would be a . . . good idea because his . . . friend in London had told him . . . a lot of . . . lies about your . . . behaviour with . . . women.''

"I am sure they are not lies,'' the *Marquis* answered,

"but when I saw you I knew you were what I had been seeking all my life and thought I would never find."

"Did you . . . really think . . . that?"

"You are the most beautiful person I have ever seen," the *Marquis* answered, "but there is so much more that at first it was impossible for me to believe you were real."

"I . . . I am very . . . real."

"I know that now, but I knew when you could read my thoughts, and I could read yours, that you were different from anybody I had ever encountered, and I knew, too, that I had to make you mine or else lose something so incredibly precious that without it I could never be a complete person."

"I . . . I thought . . . the same," Kezia whispered, "but I thought . . . you loved . . . *Madame* de Salres."

"I have never loved anyone in the real meaning of the word," the *Marquis* said firmly, "and it is going to take me a lifetime to explain to you how different what I feel for you is from anything I have ever felt before."

He drew a deep breath as if a burden had fallen from his shoulders before he said:

"How soon can we be married—tonight, tomorrow?"

Kezia gave a little cry.

"You are going so quickly . . . I want to be your wife . . . but only if you are quite . . . certain you will not be . . . bored with me."

"Bored?" the *Marquis* exclaimed. "Do you really think that is possible?"

There was a note in his voice that made her heart leap.

At the same time, she wanted to make sure that he was not making a mistake.

"You . . . realise," she said, "how . . . unsophisticated I am . . . and also . . . because I am English . . . I cannot be fascinating and amusing like . . . *Madame* de Salres."

The *Marquis* put his fingers under her chin and turned her face up to his.

"Listen, my darling one," he said, "do you really think I want my wife, and please God, the mother of my children, to be like a woman you should never have met, except that I thought your brother was a bachelor?"

He was speaking very seriously, then quite unexpectedly he laughed.

"How can you have deceived me when I pride myself on being perceptive and certainly have had enough experience to have known from the very beginning that you were not a married woman?"

"I was wearing . . . one of . . . Mama's gowns," Kezia said.

The *Marquis* smiled very tenderly.

"It was not what you were wearing, my precious," he said, "but was, I think, because I was so bemused by your beauty and by the vibrations which joined us from the first moment we met, that I found it impossible to think clearly."

He touched the softness of her cheek before he went on:

"All I knew was that my heart and soul told me I had found what I had been seeking all my life, while my brain warned me that in my position I must not be involved in a scandal."

"I think," Kezia said, "Perry expected . . . you to make . . . love to me, but thought it more . . . difficult if you were . . . staying in his house and I was his wife."

The *Marquis* thought privately that Perry had tried to make him believe he was guarding his "wife" not only in the daytime, but also at night.

He had, however, no intention of saying anything like that to Kezia.

It was her innocence and purity which had captured him in the first place.

He knew it was something so unique, so different from all the other women in whom he had been interested.

He vowed silently that he would keep her from being soiled by anything ugly or unpleasant in the Social World.

She fitted perfectly into the *Château*, where he had never brought women like *Madame* de Salres.

He had kept them in Paris or sometimes taken them to the house of his friends who were less fastidious about their homes than he was.

He had intended, in all sincerity, to leave Kezia, because she was perfect, as she was.

He was determined not to kiss her or make love to her, as he had done so many times before with so many women.

Then, when she had saved him from being crippled in a way which would have made him want to take his own life, he lost what had been an iron self-control.

He kissed her because he could not help it.

It was then he knew that without her he had no wish to go on living.

Whatever the scandal, whatever the horror and the distress to his mother and his other relations, he could not lose her.

Even if it meant he could no longer return to France, he knew that he could not give up Kezia and what she meant to him.

Now, incredibly, the miracle he had prayed for had happened.

She was free, he could marry her.

He knew with that inner perception which had been his all his life, they would be unbelievably happy together for the rest of their lives.

The enormity of it made him just sit looking at her until she asked a little anxiously:

"Have I . . . said something . . . wrong?"

"I have just decided," the *Marquis* said quietly, "that we shall be married this evening in the Chapel."

"This . . . evening?"

"I will immediately send my Secretary to the *Maire* to register our marriage as is compulsory in France."

Kezia was staring at the *Marquis* wide-eyed as he added:

"It will be the sensible thing to do. When Orvil dies, there will be a large family Funeral, but if you and I are on our honeymoon, it will be impossible for us to be present."

Then Kezia's quick brain made her understand exactly what he was telling her, and she reached out her hands saying:

"I will do . . . whatever you . . . tell me to . . . do!"

*   *   *

Kezia was in the *Boudoir* that adjoined her bedroom when Perry came in.

Because the maids were packing her clothes in her bedroom and at the same time bringing in her bath, she had undressed and put on her *négligée*.

She was standing at the window looking out at the sky.

The sun was sinking and she sent up a prayer of thankfulness to God because she was so happy.

At the same time, she was also thanking her father and mother.

"Thank you . . . thank you!" she was saying. "You have brought me the man I prayed for . . . and I know it was due to . . . you both because you were . . . helping and guiding me.''

"What is going on?" Perry asked as he came into the room. "There is no-one downstairs, but the servants tell me there has been an accident, to Orvil.''

Kezia walked across the room to him.

"Where have you been?"

Perry smiled.

"I have been in the woods with Lissette," he said, "and you must congratulate me, Kezia, for I am the happiest man in the world!"

"As I am the happiest woman!"

He looked at her in surprise and she said:

"I am being married . . . this evening to . . . the *Marquis*!"

Perry just stared at her, then he said:

"Is this a joke?"

"No, of course not," Kezia replied. "I am telling you the truth. As you have heard, the *Marquis*' brother has had an accident and we want to get away in case he dies!"

For a moment Perry was silent. Then he said:

"If he is likely to do that, knowing what the French are like when it comes to Funerals and mourning, the sooner Lissette and I leave for England, the better!"

"And . . . you will be married there?"

"Or here," Perry said, "it does not matter, as long as we do not have to wait, and she is afraid her cousin, and of course his mother, might raise objections and say we should have at least a two- or three-month engagement."

Kezia laughed.

"The *Marquis* can hardly insist on that when he is marrying me so quickly."

"No, of course not," Perry agreed, "and, Kezia, I am

really glad about it, if you are certain you know how to hold him.''

Kezia knew exactly what he was implying, and she said simply:

"Vere tells me he has been looking for me all his life. I believe him and there is no need for me to . . . say he is the . . . man of my . . . dreams.''

"I knew that you would fall in love with him!" Perry exclaimed.

"You were quite right," his sister said. "He is . . . irresistible!"

"And that is what I have to be to Lissette! Oh, Kezia, she is so adorable, and she says she will love helping me to do up the house and she does not mind being uncomfortable until we can make it perfect!''

Kezia gave a little laugh.

"Then she is exactly the right wife for you," she said, "and actually, I thought with the exception of the *Marquis* she was the nicest person in the whole party!"

"We are going to have as good if not better horses than he has," Perry boasted, "and when you come to stay with us you can compare them."

"We will do that," Kezia promised.

"I had better go now to have my bath," Perry said, walking towards the door.

Only as he reached it did he turn back to ask as an afterthought:

"By the way, I never enquired what happened to Orvil. What sort of accident did he have?"

"A pistol . . . was fired and . . . by mistake, the bullet hit . . . him," Kezia replied truthfully.

"Oh, is that all?" Perry said, and went out of the room, shutting the door behind him.

* * *

It was very quiet in the ancient Chapel when Kezia entered it on Perry's arm.

She saw the *Marquis* waiting for her.

The only other person present was Lissette, whom Perry had insisted should witness the marriage.

The *Marquis* had told Kezia just before she went down to dinner that he had decided they should be married as soon as the rest of the party had retired.

"They will not want to stay up late after what has happened," he said, "and I hear my mother and grandmother will not be coming down to dinner."

"Then we shall just be alone . . . with God," Kezia said simply.

The *Marquis* put his arms round her and drew her close to him.

"That is what I want us to be, and, my darling, when I told your brother what I had arranged, he wanted Lissette to be there, as they have decided to be married early tomorrow morning before they leave for England."

Kezia gave a little cry of delight.

"I am so glad!" she said. "I am sure Lissette will look after Perry, and make him very happy."

"I have never known a man so excited, except myself," the *Marquis* smiled, "and I have given my blessing to the marriage, which will be nearly as wonderful as ours."

"And ours will be . . . very . . . very wonderful!" Kezia said in a soft voice.

He kissed her gently.

Then he left the *Boudoir* so that they would not be seen

151

coming down the stairs together, which might cause comment amongst the servants.

*   *   *

There were eight people at dinner, and the only other woman besides Kezia and Lissette was Teresa.

She, however, complained of a headache and retired to bed soon after they had drunk their coffee in the Salon.

The men then went off to play Billiards and the two couples who wished to get married were left alone.

The *Marquis* smiled.

"What are we waiting for?"

He looked at Kezia and said:

"Go and get ready, my darling. My valet will be coming with us on our honeymoon, and is the only person in the house who knows what is taking place. He will bring you a veil which has been in my family for two hundred years."

Kezia hurried up the stairs.

She was thinking as she did so how fortunate she was that the gown she was wearing, and which the *Marquis* admitted he had chosen for her, was very suitable for a bride.

It was the one she had worn the first night, with the beautifully embroidered bertha.

The shimmering satin was exactly the same colour as the exquisite lace veil, which had yellowed very slightly with age.

She put it over her hair, then held it in place with a magnificent diamond tiara which the *Marquis* had also sent her.

It had been made by a superlative craftsman of jewellery during the reign of Louis XIV and was fashioned of flowers,

152

which made it, Kezia thought, very suitable for the *Château*.

She had never worn a tiara before.

When she looked at herself in the mirror she knew it was all part of being in the Fairy Tale that had been hers since she had crossed the Channel in the *Marquis'* yacht.

When she had her first sight of the *Château* with its five fountains throwing their glittering water towards the sky, she thought she was dreaming.

As soon as she was ready, Perry was waiting to escort her from her room down a side staircase, so that she would not be seen by the servants in the hall.

When they reached the long corridor which led to the Chapel which was at the back of the *Château*, there was a bouquet of lilies-of-the-valley waiting for her on a chair.

She knew the *Marquis* had chosen it because her room at home was the Lily-of-the-Valley-Room.

She thought only he, with his perceptive mind and attention to detail, could have remembered such a thing.

Only his brilliant organisation would have produced it at the right moment.

She was not surprised to find that in the few hours that had elapsed since he had decided they should be married this evening, the Chapel had been decorated with white flowers.

With a large number of candles lighting the altar, it was as beautiful as everything else that belonged to the *Marquis*.

He was standing waiting for her.

Since dinner he had added to his evening coat his decorations. He wore a ribbon across his shoulder and a diamond cross beneath his white tie.

The organ was playing very softly.

As the Service proceeded and the *Marquis* put a gold

ring on Kezia's finger, she knew that the angels were singing above them.

The music they heard came also from their hearts, and the song was part of themselves and the light that throbbed within them.

When the Chaplain blessed them, she knew she had been blessed already in finding love when she had thought it impossible.

Because they were so attuned to each other, she knew the *Marquis* was thinking the same thing and thanking God that his search was now over.

When finally they rose from their knees, the *Marquis* took Kezia down the short aisle and out of the Chapel.

They went up the staircase on which she had descended.

There was no-one to see them go, not into her room, but into the *Marquis'*.

It was even more magnificent than she had expected.

But she had eyes only for her husband, who for the moment did not touch her, but only stood looking at her.

"You are mine!" he said at last. "Mine from now until eternity!"

Instinctively Kezia moved nearer to him, but he did not kiss her.

Instead, he took the tiara from her head, then surprisingly he took a step backwards to look at her.

"Now you are like a Saint," he said, "and, my darling, I am ready to kneel at your feet and worship you!"

"I would . . . rather be in . . . your arms!" Kezia whispered.

He pulled her against him and asked:

"How could I have imagined that I should find you when I had decided that because you did not exist I would never marry?"

"And I . . . thought," Kezia said, "that because we were so . . . poor and I never saw any . . . men except Perry . . . I should never have . . . the chance of . . . falling in love!"

"And now the miracle has happened," the *Marquis* said, "and we are together."

He spoke so seriously that Kezia thought the vows he had made in the Chapel were still in his mind.

Then as if he were suddenly conscious of his Norman blood, he pulled Kezia close to him and kissed her demandingly.

Once again she was thinking of the wonder of it.

Her whole body was so completely merged with his that she was hardly aware when he removed her veil, then her gown, and dropped them on the ground.

Only when he lifted her up in his arms did she give a little murmur because she was shy and hid her face against his shoulder.

He set her down against the pillows in the enormous carved bed with its crimson curtains and gilded pillars.

It was very large, and as she looked up at the canopy overhead and beyond it the exquisitely painted ceiling, she felt rather small and lost.

A second later the *Marquis* joined her.

He pulled her into his arms, and she knew then that this was the dream she had always wanted to dream.

She was safe and enveloped in the love which joined her heart, her mind to his mind, her body to his body.

"I love you . . . I love you!" she whispered. "Oh, darling, wonderful Vere . . . I love you with . . . all of . . . me!"

"I adore and worship you," he said, "and, Heart of my Heart, it is something we will never lose, for our love will grow greater year by year. When we die we will be together, and nothing, not even death, can separate us."

Kezia knew that the way he spoke came from his soul.

He felt her body quiver against his and knew he had found the perfection which all men seek in life, but are so often disappointed.

Then he was kissing her; kissing her until they were flying in the sky.

The heat of the sun was burning in them both, and the Divine Light covered them as if the stars had fallen down.

* * *

A long time after, when the candles in the gold chandeliers beside the bed were guttering low, Kezia moved against the *Marquis'* shoulder.

"Are you awake, my precious?" he asked.

"I am too . . . happy to . . . sleep," she answered. "I . . . I did not realize that . . . love was so . . . wonderful . . . so different from anything I expected."

"What did you expect?" the *Marquis* asked.

"Something . . . soft and gentle . . . like the music of the bees and scent of the flowers."

The *Marquis* pulled her a little closer.

"And what is it like now?"

"It is . . . fierce . . . demanding . . . and it is . . . impossible not to be . . . conquered by it," she whispered.

"I have not frightened or hurt you?"

"No . . . of course not, but I did not expect making love to be . . . quite so . . . overwhelming or so . . . utterly and completely . . . wonderful!"

"This is only the beginning," the *Marquis* promised. "I have so much to teach you and so much to learn myself."

"What can . . . I teach . . . you?"

"You can teach me about beauty, and as you are the

most beautiful person I have ever seen, it should not be difficult. You can teach me to understand people as you do, to be compassionate, and to be concerned with their difficulties and problems, as I have tried to be in the past.''

His lips were against her cheek as he finished:

''But it was difficult with no-one beside me to help and guide me, as I know you will do in the future.''

Kezia felt the tears come into her eyes.

''How can you say . . . anything so . . . marvellous to . . . me?'' she asked. ''It makes me feel . . . very humble . . . after all . . . as you know . . . I am very inexperienced . . . and perhaps rather . . . foolish.''

''You are very wise in the things that really matter, the things I have been looking for, but alone.''

Kezia put her arm protectively across his chest, and said:

''Now I know why, although you are strong and omnipotent, I want to . . . protect . . . you. I want to prevent anything from . . . hurting you either physically or spiritually. At the same time . . . I feel safe because you will . . . look after me.''

The *Marquis* gave a deep sigh.

''How is it possible,'' he asked, ''that after all the sins I have committed, and there have been a number of them, God sent me anything as wonderful as you?''

He kissed her forehead before he went on:

''Like the Star of Bethlehem I shall follow you in the future in so many ways, and yet, as you said, I will look after you and protect you, and if any man comes near you or tries to take you from me, I swear I will kill him!''

He spoke so fiercely that Kezia laughed.

''There speaks the Norman! But you are quite safe, my darling, there is . . . no man in the . . . whole world who could look like you . . . speak like you . . . or feel like . . . you."

"That is what I want to believe," the *Marquis* said.

He turned towards her, leaning on his elbow.

She thought he would kiss her, but for the moment he just looked down at her.

"Tomorrow," he said, "we are leaving on a voyage of discovery to find our real selves which we have always hidden from the world because they were too intimate, too precious."

Kezia was listening as he went on:

"But now we are joined together we will make one complete person, and that is what, my lovely, perfect little wife, we are going to be—a complete person."

His hand touched her breast and he went on:

"An example to all those who have sought as we have for the love which is different, the love which when one finds it is perfect."

His lips sought Kezia's.

When she could speak again she said:

"Do you . . . realise, darling, that all this has . . . happened because you . . . wanted to buy a necklace that caused a . . . great deal of unhappiness . . . not only for the people . . . involved with it . . . but to France?"

"A necklace which I will never allow you to wear," the *Marquis* replied, "but I will, however, always treasure it, because it brought me to you."

Then he said:

"But I will buy you a necklace of diamonds, and of several other stones with which to express my love."

Kezia laughed, and it was a very happy sound.

"I would much . . . rather have . . . a necklace of . . . your kisses, and that will be . . . a present for which I will be . . . greedy enough to want not once . . . but many . . . times!''

"It is a present you shall have!" the *Marquis* answered.

He kissed her forehead, her eyes, her little straight nose, but when her lips were waiting for his he bent and kissed her neck.

She did not realise in her innocence that it would awake in her different feelings from those she had ever felt before.

As his lips journeyed slowly over the softness of her skin she felt a flame like the burning heat of the sun moving through her body, into her breasts, and up to her lips.

Her breath came quickly between her lips, and she stirred beneath him.

"Does that excite my darling?" he asked.

"It makes . . . me feel . . . strange."

"In what way?"

"Very . . . very . . . thrilled and . . ."

Her voice died away.

"And . . . ?"

"Perhaps you will . . . be . . . shocked!"

"Tell me."

"I feel . . . wild . . . almost madly excited . . . is that . . . wrong?"

"Wrong! My precious, my adorable, perfect, innocent little wife, it is right and what I want you to feel. This is love, my darling—real love."

"Oh . . . Verc!"

It was a cry of inexpressible joy.

Then as the *Marquis* completed the circle at the base of her throat she quivered with an ecstasy that swept through her whole body.

Until, as his mouth took possession of hers, there was

the music of angels, the light of God, and they were one person.

Complete, perfect, in the love that was beauty itself, and was theirs for Eternity.

ABOUT THE AUTHOR

Barbara Cartland, the world's most famous romantic novelist, who is also an historian, playwright, lecturer, political speaker and television personality, has now written over 506 books and sold over 500 million copies all over the world.

She has also had many historical works published and has written four autobiographies as well as the biographies of her mother and that of her brother, Ronald Cartland, who was the first Member of Parliament to be killed in the last war. This book has a preface by Sir Winston Churchill and has just been republished with an introduction by Sir Arthur Bryant.

Love at the Helm, a novel written with the help and inspiration of the late Earl Mountbatten of Burma, Great Uncle of His Royal Highness The Prince of Wales, is being sold for the Mountbatten Memorial Trust.

She has broken the world record for the last fourteen years by writing an average of twenty-three books a year. In the *Guinness Book of Records* she is listed as the world's top-selling author.

Miss Cartland in 1978 sang an Album of Love Songs with the Royal Philharmonic Orchestra.

In private life Barbara Cartland, who is a Dame of the Order of St. John of Jerusalem, Chairman of the St. John Council in Hertfordshire and Deputy President of the St. John Ambulance Brigade, has fought for better conditions and salaries for Midwives and Nurses.

She championed the cause for the Elderly in 1956 invoking a Government Enquiry into the "Housing Conditions of Old People."

In 1962 she had the Law of England changed so that Local Authorities had to provide camps for their own Gypsies. This has meant that since then thousands and thousands of Gypsy children have been able to go to School, which they had never been able to do in the past, as their caravans were moved every twenty-four hours by the Police.

There are now fourteen camps in Hertfordshire and Barbara Cartland has her own Romany Gypsy Camp called Barbaraville by the Gypsies.

Her designs "Decorating with Love" are being sold all over the U.S.A. and the National Home Fashions League made her, in 1981, "Woman of Achievement."

She is unique in that she was one and two in the Dalton list of Best Sellers, and one week had four books in the top twenty.

Barbara Cartland's book *Getting Older, Growing Younger* has been published in Great Britain and the U.S.A. and her fifth cookery book, *The Romance of Food*, is now being used by the House of Commons.

In 1984 she received at Kennedy Airport America's Bishop Wright Air Industry Award for her contribution to the development of aviation. In 1931 she and two R.A.F. Officers thought of, and carried, the first aeroplane-towed glider airmail.

During the War she was Chief Lady Welfare Officer in Bedfordshire looking after 20,000 Service men and women. She thought of having a pool of Wedding Dresses at the War Office so a Service Bride could hire a gown for the day.

She bought 1,000 gowns without coupons for the A.T.S., the W.A.A.F.'s and the W.R.E.N.S. In 1945 Barbara Cartland received the Certificate of Merit from Eastern Command.

In 1964 Barbara Cartland founded the National Association for Health of which she is the President, as a front for all the Health Stores and for any product made as alternative medicine.

This is now a £500,000 turnover a year, with one third going in export.

In January 1988 she received *La Médaille de Vermeil de la Ville de Paris*. This is the highest award to be given in France by the City of Paris. She has sold 25 million books in France.

In March 1988 Barbara Cartland was asked by the Indian Government to open their health resort outside Delhi. This is almost the largest health resort in the world.

Barbara Cartland was received with great enthusiasm by her fans, who fêted her at a reception in the city and she received the gift of an embossed plate from the government.